Rebar works on making up for his mistake even though Cameo has moved on. He's determined to hold true to his values and prove whose side he's really on.

The battle with the General comes to a head. And the fallout leaves everyone shellshocked.

Bonds are broken. New bonds are formed in this intense drama of love, action and suspense!

With a Force of Eight
Copyright © 2023 Shiloh Love
ISBN: 978-1-4874-4051-0
Cover art by Martine Jardin

Published by eXtasy Books Inc

Look for us online at:
www.eXtasybooks.com

WITH A FORCE OF EIGHT FEATHER BLUE: 6

BY

SHILOH LOVE

CHAPTER ONE

*I*n the dimness of the room, she could see his menacing shadow tow-
ering over her. Tears soaked her cheeks. She glanced at the wall.
*The silhouette of his arm raised to strike again, made her cringe,
forcing her into a quivering ball huddled on the floor.*

A crack . . . his whip cut into the flesh of her back.

*His arsenal hung on the wall like trophies of conquests. If only
she could reach one.*

If only just once she could fight back.

*If only she could force herself to crawl just a couple of feet, despite
the searing pain, despite his verbal abuse echoing around her head.*

If only.

*In a momentary instant, a fleeting glimpse of a pause in time —
he stopped to switch the crop to his other hand.*

A breath.

A lunge.

A desperate grasp of hope.

*She rolled out of reach and hit the wall. He cussed and stumbled
in his attempt to corner her again. She reached up, fingers grappling
for anything to stop the horror.*

Hard cold metal.

One finger.

Two.

*She curled them around the barrel and yanked it off the wall
bracket. She knew it was loaded. They were always loaded.*

He lifted his arm threateningly, the fringed whip in his hand.

*Flashes of light, followed by rapid pops, rang out in the night.
The whip dropped to the floor. He buckled forward. She scooted out
of the way just as he went down with a heavy thud.*

1

Her stomach knotted from panic. Her mouth was dry with fear. Her fingers grasped the trigger so tightly that it cut through her flesh. Adrenaline raced through her trembling body.

Was he dead?

She summoned her last ounce of strength to dash from the room, away from his reign of terror. Outside the house, she gulped in fresh night air. Cool. Damp. Invigorating. The heavy mist soothed her burning skin, giving her a renewed burst of energy. She dropped the weapon and ran, her long legs sprinting, her bare feet churning up the dirt.

Freedom was hers tonight.

Cattle grazed peacefully in a lower pasture. A welcome sight loomed in the distance, a safe haven. She sprinted toward the ranch home, its windows aglow with soft, welcoming lights.

She slowed to a trot, then a walk. as she neared the house. A man stood on the wraparound porch, one hand slanted over his brow as he watched her crossing the front lawn.

"Halo!" He met her on the grass. "Where'd you run off to in the middle of the night? I was worried out of my mind."

"Don't you know?" She tilted her head curiously. "He had to die."

He slid a protective arm around her waist as they strolled to the porch lit by soft outdoor lights, then he turned toward her. Concern brimmed in the shadowy depths of his black eyes. He caressed her cheek with one hand.

"Who, babe? Who had to die?"

"The General. You don't have to worry now. Ricochet won't need to risk their lives going after him. I made him pay for shooting you."

He pulled her into a loving embrace. "Angel . . ." The word rolling off his tongue was laced with affection. "C'mon, girl. Let me help you back up to bed. You've had a long night."

She pulled back and stared up at him. "I had to do it, Rush.

I couldn't let him hurt anyone again."

"I know . . . I know." His voice was soft, kind, loaded with compassion, as were his eyes. "It's okay." He smiled reassuringly at her. "Let's get some sleep."

"Okay . . ." She leaned against him as they meandered into the house. "I am very tired."

Cameo woke to Texas sunlight pouring through the windows of the master bedroom. She loved Rush's home. It was bright and cheery during the day and it was cozy and safe throughout the night.

"Hey, you're finally awake," he greeted softly from the doorway.

"Sorry I slept so late. Did I miss breakfast?" She pulled on a pair of denim shorts and a white tank top over her undergarments. "Geez, I really passed out last night. Didn't even put my nightshirt on."

He picked her hairbrush off the dresser and sat beside her on the bed. "How are you feeling today?"

She shrugged while looking at her feet and legs in surprise. "Why are my feet so dirty, and I'm all scratched up?"

"You had a PTSD blackout," he replied calmly while brushing her long hair.

"I did? How do you know?"

"We were getting ready to turn in for the night. When I came out of the shower you were gone. I found you running from the lower fields back to the house."

"Oh, gosh." Heat flooded her cheeks. "I'm so sorry. My first night here and I go crazy."

He chuckled softly in an accepting manner. "No worries. We expected it eventually . . . the episodes that is."

"We?"

"Chamber, Shook . . . me. Our force of eight has helped countless women through the aftermath of trauma."

"A force of eight?" She gave him a quizzical look. "There were only four members when we rescued Malika."

Rush nodded apologetically. "We underestimated the old man. Didn't think one old geezer and his two wacko daughters would put up such a tough fight. This time we'll be going in with what we call our Force of Eight, our extreme team."

"When will I meet this elite force?"

"They were going to ride in last night, but I asked them to hold off until today."

"Because of me?" she asked, struggling to recall something, anything, from her blackout.

He shrugged casually. "They understand. You've been through hell. It's what we do, remember? Nobody gets left behind once we're involved. We ensure all victims we've rescued have support systems in place." He added a few more delicate sweeps of the brush to her hair, gazing adoringly at her. "I'm glad you decided to bunk here with me and didn't stay in Denver to deal with this alone."

"Strange," she said. "I really thought I was okay. That I could handle the fallout on my own. Thank you for looking out for me."

He laid the brush aside and skimmed a kiss along her cheek. "Promise you'll talk to me if you start to remember the blackout, okay?"

She nodded. "Did I say anything to you about it?"

"A little. It would be best if I let your mind process the flashback at its own pace."

"So, I was roaming around with the cows, acting crazy, huh?" She scoffed.

He laughed a little at her wit. "You're not alone. We've seen almost everything in the work that we do. Crazy doesn't scare us."

"You're a real sweetheart, you know that?" She turned to him and wrapped both arms around his neck. "You have this quiet strength about you that makes me feel calm."

"That's a good thing." He placed a kiss on her lips. "Are you hungry? We can grab lunch."

"Ah. I did miss breakfast then."

"I didn't want to wake you. The guys will be rolling in this evening. Do you feel up to it?"

"Yes. Definitely," she replied. "I can't wait to meet this force of eight."

A pleased smile curved his sexy lips. "They'll adore you, just like I do." He stood and pulled her off the bed. "C'mon, my wandering angel, there's a good steakhouse not far from here with an awesome lunch menu."

"Am I dressed okay?" She pulled her hair to one side and straightened it.

"You look beautiful. Don't worry so much. You'll fit in just fine." His adoring gaze swept over her. "Do you eat meat?"

Sudden awkwardness washed through her. "I know. I look anorexic. I have a high metabolism. Yes, I eat practically anything. I'm a little self-conscious about how skinny I am."

"Don't be. You're a fox." He gave her a sexy wink.

She felt herself blush and offered him a grateful smile. "Let's go put some meat on my bones, then," she said with a light laugh.

He chuckled at her pun. "Have I told you how happy I am that you're staying with me?"

"Yes." She giggled. "But I don't mind hearing it again."

"I usually take my Harley everywhere but if you'd rather go by car, I have one of those in the garage."

"Oooh, what do you have? I'm a bit of a muscle car fan, as you might know."

He nodded. "Your Gran Sport makes a statement, for sure."

"She is sweet. What do you drive?"

"Well . . . it's not as flashy as your hotrod, but I have a

sixty-nine Mercury Montego MX."

"Really?" Her interest piqued. "I would love to see it. I had a Shelby ya know."

"I heard you traded it for the Gran Sport."

"Yeah. I think she got the higher-end car but my Gran Sport is rare. Chamber challenged me with his Hemi Cuda." She laughed. "That will be a fun race. I hope he enjoys washing his car cause he'll see nothing but dust."

Rush laughed. "You're a wild one."

She looked up at him and smiled but didn't respond to his latter comment. "Show me your Montego! That's, after I use the bathroom. Where is it?"

He pointed at a door. "Ensuite is there. I'll wait for you in the hallway."

She quickly took care of business, then went to the fancy sink and washed her face, arms, legs, and feet. For lack of her toothbrush, she rinsed her mouth with the mouthwash that stood on the counter, then quickly left the bathroom to join him.

They strolled out the back door, across the patio, and past a grand swimming pool, then down a sloping stone walk to a huge metal building. Rush opened a side door and waved her in ahead of him.

"Wow . . ." She sighed, feeling impressed while gawking around. "This place is immaculate. Didn't look like much from the outside."

"With all the storms we get, I don't fuss over the exterior. I'm constantly replacing the siding. But the building is sturdy enough to protect what's inside and that's what counts."

She wandered around the huge storage, admiring his impressive collection of cars. "I had no idea you were a car buff."

"Had me pegged as just a biker, huh?" he teased.

"Kinda. Actually, I never gave it much thought. I figured since most of Ricochet ride Harleys, and you being their leader . . ." Her voice trailed off as he led her to a gleaming black, head-turning, Mercury Montego MX. Immediately she spotted the cobra badge on the front fender just before the door. "A Cobra Jet?" She cast him an inquisitive look.

"Four-twenty-eight," he replied proudly, then popped the hood.

"Mercy," she said on an airy breath. "I see why you use the Harley for missions. This beauty is pristine."

"Thanks." He slid behind the wheel and fired up the engine.

Cameo stepped back in awe. Nothing sounded better than a ripping V8 coursing through duel Flowmaster exhaust — the gutsy growly rumble that let everyone know you've got power under the hood. She jumped in on the passenger side and slid across the black leather bench seat.

"Omigosh, this is such a classy car." She snuggled next to him, looping her arm through his.

He tapped the button on the visor to open the garage door with a big grin on his face. "Feels loads better with a hot lady at my side. I knew these bench seats would be good for something."

"Mm. I can think of a few ideas."

"Are you flirting with me, girl?"

"Do you mind?"

"Hell, no. I love it." He guided the car down his mile-long driveway then onto the road. "I love your straightforward nature."

"Thanks. I don't know any other way to be." She eyed up the sleek interior. "Custom sound system. Do you mind if I play music? Can you roll the windows down? I love blasting tunes and flying down the highway with the wind in my hair."

"Go for it, sugar. You're my kinda gal."

She pulled a Classic Rock CD from his stack and slipped it

into the player then turned the volume up. Rush was still grinning as they flew down the highway. She thought about how all of Tassos' sons were into cars. But she'd never say that to him. Never openly compare him to the two brothers he never knew he had until just recently. His decision to keep his paternity a secret would forever be safe with her.

A fast, exhilarating, short drive brought them to a Texas steakhouse. Rush parked on the far side of the lot away from all other cars. She understood. The best place to get scratches on one's car was in a parking lot.

Mid July weather was warm, a bit muggy with plenty of sunshine. He held her hand as they went inside and got seated. A pretty little waitress wearing a halter top, short shorts and ankle boots, took their order.

"Anything else, Rush?" she asked.

Cameo was surprised the server addressed him by name, yet she refrained from commenting for fear of sounding jealous.

"That's all," he replied.

There didn't appear to be any flirting between them, for which she was glad.

Cameo took in her surroundings. She wasn't overly fond of the décor. Massive steer heads were mounted to the walls, horns and all. Other western regalia was placed randomly throughout. She ignored the blatant display of man over mammal and sipped a cold drink.

"You haven't said a word since we hit the road," Rush noted. "Everything okay?"

"Just getting used to more changes," she replied. "This drink tastes great. I wonder if they made it from fresh lemons or if it's a mix."

"This place makes everything from scratch so I would guess it's real lemonade. That's why I like coming here. I'm not much for cooking, but I do love a homemade meal."

"I figured you were a regular here."

"I hope that doesn't make you feel awkward. All the waitresses know me."

"Nope. I have no claims on you. And it's not like you were ogling each other in front of me, so it's cool."

He draped an arm over her shoulder and leaned in close. "Angel, I have eyes only for you."

"Was there ever a Mrs. Rush Levvy?" she boldly asked.

"No. Never married. My work with Ricochet and other projects kept me plenty busy." He paused to take a swig of his beer, then added, "I'm not the skirt-chaser type. How about you? Ever married?"

"No. Got close once or twice. Like you, I have interests other than the opposite sex. I wasn't even thinking about dating when Rebar chased me down."

"I remember you telling me about that. I'm not him, though. You and I met by fate, not because I cornered you into dating me."

She smiled. "It does feel like fate, doesn't it? Even the little angel girl. Everything that's happened with you just kinda flowed naturally."

"Yeah." He stroked her hair while gazing at her with those smoky eyes. "And it'll continue that way if we let it. Just be, babe, just be. Let go of the whole sibling dramas we have in our lives. I'll never compare you to Camille and I know you'll never compare me to Rebar or Shade. I'm nothing like them, and from what I've heard about Camille and briefly saw of her, you are nothing like your twin."

"You're right." She touched his handsome face. "Everything does feel natural with you . . . and easy."

"Now that's what I like to hear." He dropped a quick sweet kiss on her lips. "Through Ricochet I know people from many different places. A lot of them are women because of what we do. Try not to feel threatened if we encounter them from time to time, okay?"

"Okay. I'm really not the jealous type. Well, maybe a little." She scoffed. "I was jealous over Rebar and Camille."

"Seems to me you had reason."

"Yeah." She sighed. "I should've followed through on my gut feeling from the start . . . run. But I did run, and he chased. And Malika knew all this yet remained silent on her intent. So damn frustrating."

"Well, you have a clean slate with me, and likewise. We have no prior connections to get in the way."

The waitress arrived with their order. Camille stared at the massive bun on her plate loaded with shaved Ribeye, cheese, and an array of veggies, plus fries. She was glad the food arrived before she started rattling on about her feelings.

"I'm not sure I can eat all this in one sitting," she said. "There's enough sandwich here to feed four."

"Just do the best you can. We can take what's left home." He dug into his with zeal.

Cameo slid a French fry off the sandwich and nibbled on it. The flavor was spicy. She scraped the fries off then tried to get her mouth around the burger. After several tries from different angles, she managed to take a good bite.

"Don't like the fries?" he asked.

"Sorry. They taste peppery."

"No worries. Just dump 'em on my plate if you don't want 'em."

She held her plate over his. "Have at it."

He slid the fries onto his plate and resumed eating. She couldn't help but remember eating Rebar's special Ramen recipe. He was such a gentle soul and she'd thought they had a lot in common.

Right now, she felt very out of place. This was clearly Rush's stomping ground. He even knew the servers. She'd dined in the finest and the worst places, but the staff never addressed her by her first name. This culture differed greatly from what she was accustomed to. She began to worry that she might not fit in Rush's world.

Their physical chemistry was off the charts. But what if they didn't have enough in common to build a relationship? She decided to keep her heart in check. After all, she was still on the rebound, and a daunting task lay ahead.

By the time Rush had finished his meal, she was still picking hers apart, eating the parts she liked. The steak was chewy, so she carefully pushed it aside. The cheese was also spicy, like nacho or something. And the veggies were heavily seasoned. She didn't want to insult his favorite eatery so she ate what she could. Anxiety crept over her. She chugged the lemonade and asked for a refill.

"Would you care for dessert?" the waitress asked. "And a takeout bag?"

Cameo looked over the dessert menu and chose chocolate lava cake. *A safe bet,* she thought. *They can't ruin chocolate cake.* Rush passed on dessert but accepted another beer. Other than a strong physical resemblance, she'd never guess he was Rebar's half-brother. They had entirely different auras and tastes.

In all fairness, Rush had told her straight up that he wasn't refined like his two brothers. She began to see he hadn't lied. He was a true roughneck in every sense. She envisioned him wrestling cattle, sitting around a fire drinking with friends and doing all the typical things country guys did.

"What time is Ricochet coming in tonight?" she asked while eating the cake.

He leaned back in his chair, staring intently at her. "I don't know. They'll show when they show. How's the cake?"

"Okay." She wrinkled her brows at him. "Is something wrong?"

"You really didn't like the food here, did you?"

She hesitated then shook her head. "I'm sorry."

He laughed, as if amused. "Don't be. This place is a dive. I just wanted to test your authenticity."

Her eyes widened in surprise. "But *you* ate it, heartily!"

"I'll eat anything. After the things I've seen. I never waste food. But this grub does taste like shit."

She playfully swatted him. "I can't believe you did this! I was actually hungry."

"I'm sorry," he said, laughing. "I had to see your reaction. You're such a proper lady with an impressive resume and upbringing. I had to see if you were a snob or not."

"You are such a scoundrel."

"Yeah . . . I am." He was still grinning. "Glad to see you are a good sport about it. How about we grab a pizza on the way back?"

"Are you going to set me up with that, too?" she teased.

"I don't know. Do you like anchovies, hot peppers and onions on yours?"

"Nooo, and if you do, don't plan on kissing me tonight."

Rush paid the check, left a generous tip and escorted her from the restaurant. "Just messing with you, sugar. Tell me what you want to eat and I'll get it."

"I love a good sub sandwich and pizza, but nothing too spicy."

He opened the driver's side door and gestured for her to get in. She slid to the middle as he slipped behind the wheel. "What's your comfort food? Be honest."

"Ice cream and noodles," she confessed. "And soup."

"Gotcha."

He drove her to a grocery store on the way back and told her to load the cart with whatever she wanted.

"Remember, I don't cook, I only grill," he said as they bagged the items.

"I can cook, if you don't mind me working in that gorgeous

kitchen of yours."

"I'd love to smell food coming from that kitchen again. I'm sure my grandmother and great-grandmother would be delighted to see their kitchen back in use."

"You haven't used it?" She shot him an incredulous look. "At all?"

"Nope. And I've never had a woman stay with me either. You'll be the first. You okay with that? I'm not making you feel too domestic or anything, am I?"

"You?" She laughed outright. "No, no. I don't get that feeling from you at all. I picture you quite differently."

"How so?" He loaded all the bags into one hand.

She couldn't help but notice his bulging biceps and the memory of those strong arms holding her whipped through her mind. There was no denying the physical attraction she felt for him, besides the chemistry that lurked between them. "Roping cows, drinking around a fire."

"Okay . . . cow roping." He laughed. "That's almost cruel. But drinking around a fire. Hell, yeah. That's what we'll be doing tonight with the guys. Not afraid to get a little grass on your ass, are ya, sweetheart?"

"Ha. You know I'm not. I trudged through dust and dirt with you, caked with blood."

"Good. Cuz I love chilling around a fire at night and doing some star gazing. Texas has a gorgeous sky. There are millions of stars to look at. The beauty of nature never ceases to amaze me."

She watched him load the bags into the spacious carpeted trunk of his Montego. He'd done a complete one-eighty on her, catching her off guard.

This man intrigued her. She began looking forward to knowing him on a deeper level.

CHAPTER TWO

Flames reached high into the night sky, crackling, as the blaze consumed their quarry of wood and dried branches.

Rush tossed a blanket on the grass. "That's in case we wanna get cozy," he told her with a spirited wink. "Can't get that night in Santa Fe outta my mind."

She sashayed over to him and slid both arms around his neck. "Neither can I." She stood on tip toes to reach up and kiss him. "It's beautiful out here at night. I'll try not to wander away this time."

"I'll keep you close." His arms encircled her waist. "Especially tonight with the guys here."

"You're silly. I'm sure they all have girlfriends or wives. Besides, I'm not a rock star. I'm a skinny blonde with a dark past. Not exactly every man's dream."

He brushed his lips against hers. "You're *my* dream come true."

His flattery charmed her. Few men had impressed her with wit, resilience, and sweettalk.

"Just don't let me roam with the cows again tonight, please. I'm afraid of another blackout."

"It's good that you admit that to me. Most victims go into denial. Your realistic attitude about the past and your present situation is the first step toward healing. And you're stoic as hell. I really admire you."

"Thank you," she said with a modest smile. "But I actually *am* afraid. I've never gone AWOL that I know of. How will I know when I'm better?"

"You'll know. But until then, I'm here. And Chamber will be around, too. Not sure how long the others will hang out, but they're all trained at various levels to help post trauma victims."

"Ricochet sounds amazing."

"I think we are," came a voice from the shadows.

Rush and Cameo turned at the same time. "Hey, Shook," he said in greeting. "You made it. Where's your . . . significant other?"

"Not far from here in a hotel up in Plano." Shook walked up to them. He was barely an inch shorter than Rush. Shiny black hair framed his face and hung to his collar in wavy layers. He gave Cameo a hard once over with penetrating black eyes. "How ya doing, Halo? Haven't seen you since Raton."

"Hanging in there," she replied shyly. "How are you? I heard you're keeping strange company these days."

He laughed a little then nodded. "Sorry about that. But someone's gotta keep tabs on Malika, and she zeroed in on me. Looks like I'm it."

"Please be careful. She's ruthless." Cameo warned.

"Don't worry, babe. We know what we're doing." He walked to the cooler and reached in for an iced-down brew.

She heard the grass crunching as more people approached. Rush watched quietly as the men filtered in and grabbed a cold bottle before gathering around.

"Where's Hunter?" he asked.

"Down under," Levi replied.

Cameo remembered Levi from their run to Raton. His striking blue eyes and straight black hair were a unique contrast. He had an easygoing smile and wore his hair pulled back into a long ponytail. He still had the same evening shadow as the last time she'd seen him, or maybe that was his permanent look, she decided.

Moss walked up beside him and gave her a polite nod. He

was wearing a spiked collar around his neck, and leather wrist cuffs. His medium brown hair had a lovely light curl to it and fell past the collar of his leather jacket. Facial hair formed a short neatly trimmed beard around his chin, jaw, and upper lip.

All the members of Ricochet were tall with dark hair in various shades, except Chamber who was the only blond. Every man in the group was built to the max, muscled and strong in appearance. There were a couple of guys present that she'd never met.

"Cameo, let's get you acquainted," said Rush. He pointed slightly toward them as everyone stood in a casual circle close together. "You know Moss, Levi and Shook. Although, I'm not sure I even recognize Moss tonight with the dog collar," he joked.

"Hey, this is my battle mode attire," Moss retorted with a grin.

Rush shook his head and smiled. "That character over there with the kinky long hair, wearing a do-rag is Stoke. And the dude beside him with even longer hair and no headwrap who looks like Count Dracula, is Rider."

"Don't worry, Halo. I won't bite unless you ask," Rider said with a wink.

She was glad for the cover of night to hide her heating cheeks.

Stoke offered his hand in greeting. "Nice to meet you, Halo. We've heard you're quite the warrior."

"Nice to meet you, too." She accepted his hand.

Her gaze moved discreetly around the group, sizing up each man. Not an ugly one in the pack. Handsome faces, some of them more rugged, with very short circle beards that could alternately be considered heavy evening shadows. *Perhaps the men don't bother to shave while on the road.* And not one of them had short hair, some wore their hair longer especially Stoke and Rider. She'd never seen those two. They looked tough.

"Did Hunter get my message?" Rush asked.

"We don't know. He's been down under on assignment for weeks. He might be in the outback," Rider told him. "Nobody's heard from him in a while."

"We need eight. Nobody goes in without a wingman." Rush became quiet.

"I hear ya," Stoke agreed. "We can't let another warrior take a bullet from that prick."

Just then, Chamber strolled into the firelight. His long blond hair shone in the flickering glow. "Hey, mates!"

Then a very familiar face appeared at his side. Cameo covered her mouth and gasped as the two approached.

"I heard that Hunter can't make it. I happened to run into a fill-in if Rush approves," Chamber said.

Standing across from her, wearing his favorite leather jacket and black jeans, was Rebar. She couldn't fathom why Chamber would do this to her. Tears sprang to her eyes. She held them back. Just the sight of him brought back a flood of hurt.

"What the hell is he doing here?" snapped Rush.

"Just hear me out, mate. Okay?" Chamber implored.

"He's got a mouth. Let *him* tell me."

Chamber gave a nod of respect and took a step back. "The floor is yours, Rebar."

Rush glared at him. Lines on his face tightened. "And you've got about two minutes to convince me why I shouldn't throw your ass off my property."

"I want to help," Rebar began. "I'm not here to cause trouble. I drove down alone and called Chamber. Asked him to bring me along so I could try and earn your acceptance. I couldn't stay with Camille after I heard her plotting with Malika. In that moment, she and her mother became the same person to me. My loyalty is here. I rode with most of you to

Raton. I utilized my secret tracking device to help. I severed ties with Shade and his troop to help stop the General. And even when I ended up alone after screwing up, I still didn't want to rejoin forces with him. When I met Ricochet, I felt like I'd finally found the family I never had. I was never close to Shade. Chamber can vouch for that. And I don't wanna be. I don't like the man he's become, nor do I condone what Camille is doing."

Rush rubbed his chin while listening intently. His comrades waited and watched in pensive silence. Cameo observed every man standing in that circle—even Rebar. She struggled to remain composed, wondering how Rush would react.

"What's your current status with Camille?"

"I'm done with her. She's not the person I thought she was. I was caught up in some kind of fantasy."

"Does she know you're *done*?"

Rebar nodded once. "I made it unmistakably clear and told her she best make amends with Shade. She stormed out. I'm not sure if she went back to Shade or went to stay with her mother. But I really don't care. I don't share my life with liars or thieves."

"One more question," Rush said. "Did you come here to make another play for Cameo?"

"I won't deny I'm still in love with her," Rebar replied, briefly glancing her way. "I never stopped loving her. But I'm not going to cause her more stress than I already have. Chamber set me straight on that. I really need to be near my best friend right now, and I want to become a respected member of your family."

"We actually do have an opening at the moment since Hunter is MIA. You do realize that the seven of us will be your worst enemies if you step out of line, especially regarding Cameo."

"I hear you loud and clear." Rebar showed nothing but respect toward Rush. "I'm willing to do whatever it takes to make up for my stupidity."

Rush shifted his focus to Chamber. "You know him better than anyone. Tell me straight, can we believe what he just said?"

"Yeah, man," Chamber replied. "I'd never have brought him to your home if I had any doubt. He's one of the good guys and like a brother to me. Always has been. He got caught up in Shade and Camille's twisted game. I really think he needs a few good friends right now."

"You trust him to be your wingman?" Rush asked point blank.

Chamber didn't hesitate. "Yep. I know he'll have my back."

Cameo glared at Chamber. "How could you do this? You came into my apartment and pretended to care about me. Called me on the phone. Persuaded me into giving you my location. Then you drag Rebar right into my face? You manipulated me just to help your best buddy?"

"Cameo, no!" refuted Chamber. "I was sincere every minute I was with you. Rebar didn't catch up with me until this morning. I swear I didn't know he was coming."

"Yeah, right," she spat. "Like you didn't clue him in as to where you were headed. I'm not naïve. I actually started to trust you."

"No, darlin', I'd never deceive you in any way."

"Don't *darlin'* me!" She stalked across the circle and backhanded him across the face. "Don't ever pretend to be my friend again." With that, she pushed past him and ran toward the house.

Once inside, she hurried to the freezer, grabbed a pint of ice cream and a spoon then dashed to the bedroom. Curled up on the bed, she dug into the ice cream and cried.

Rush must've been right behind her because he entered the

bedroom seconds later and closed the door. "Hey, angel, I'm sorry they upset you."

"Doesn't matter. You're all men. A tightknit group of friends. You always look out for one another."

"Yeah we do. But you're my top priority right now. If you want Rebar to leave, I'll send him off. I can't boot Chamber, though. He's been with us from the beginning. Did something happen between the two of you? Why are you this upset over Chamber? If he mistreated you, I'll handle it."

"He didn't do anything wrong, except maybe mislead me by flirting. He showed up at my apartment in Denver after the breakup and pretended to care about me. He actually made me smile. He made me believe Ricochet was looking out for me."

"We are, babe. I've known Chamber a long time. He's a hopeless flirt but he wouldn't deliberately mislead you."

She looked up at him through teary eyes. "You're okay with him bringing Rebar here, and asking that he become part of the family after what he did to me?"

"Not really. The man's still in love with you. But I'm not insecure. I'm trying to be objective. I've always considered myself a fair-minded man."

"What can Rebar possibly have to contribute to your pack? His inventions?"

Rush slid in beside her and wrapped an arm around her shoulders. "He can be Chamber's wingman. Our teams are Levi and Moss, Rider and Stoke, Chamber and Hunter, me and Shook. Hunter's out of touch. Maybe this is a good thing. I look out for every member of my family. Since Shook will be floating between us and Malika, I'm able to take you with me. It's not fair to leave Chamber without a wingman."

"What if Hunter returns?"

"We can't risk losing track of the General by waiting on Hunter." He grimaced. "I don't even know if he got my text, and Australia isn't around the corner. We can't sit around waiting. Do you think I'm gonna let that bastard General get away with what he did to you? This is the first time we've actually zeroed in on the man's location, all because of you. I don't want your suffering to be in vain."

"I know. I get that. But Rebar? Seriously?"

"Not the ideal situation, for sure. On the upside, what a better way to get over him than to show him he didn't destroy you. That you have another guy who's crazy about you."

"Aren't you the least bit worried that I might go back to Rebar?" she asked with scrunched up brows. "You said it yourself, I'm on the rebound. I'm not over him yet."

Rush let out a heavy sigh. "Yeah . . . I'd be a fool not to worry a little. I've seen women run back to men years after they got free. I won't control you. And I really don't want to hide our relationship and lose precious time out of fear. You're either gonna go back to the man or not. No amount of time will change that. But I'm a risktaker, and you're definitely worth the risk."

"Do you think I'll weaken and go back? He can be quite persuasive." Knowing her heart, she was genuinely worried over this.

Rush visibly contemplated her question, then replied. "No. You're a smart lady. Honest, loyal . . . and most of all, I believe you'll always be true to yourself. I don't know the dynamics of your relationship with him, but something was off-kilter for you to end up in my arms that night. I'm guessing that no matter what he says or does, you'll always wonder in the back of that beautiful mind of yours if he's still in love with Camille."

She pondered his reply while eating her ice cream. He sat patiently next to her, simply caressing her arms with his fingertips as he liked to do. He seemed streetwise and extremely intuitive.

"Another thing I picked up on," Rush added in a soft voice. "You were quickly getting attached to Chamber. Maybe too attached. You really let him have it. I'm guessing he flirted with you quite a bit by the way you belted him."

"You're very perceptive. Either that or you know his MO."

"Chamber never stays in one place too long. He has girlfriends all over the world. I'm sorry he led you on while you were most vulnerable. I'll have a word with him."

"Are you upset that I was getting attached to him?" She stabbed at her ice cream. "I even shared my last pint of comfort food with him."

"Nah. I could never be upset with you. I do feel bad that he wasn't more tactful, especially knowing your fragile state of mind. Seems he needs a reminder of what we do." He peered into the almost empty ice cream carton. "You shared your last pint with Chamber yet sat here and chowed that down without even offering me a bite?" He feigned a wounded look and flattened one hand over his heart. "That's ice cold, baby." He grinned slightly.

"Ha-ha, cute pun." She giggled and playfully pouted, then scooped a nice, rounded bite onto the spoon and offered it to him.

He wrapped his lips around the spoon and pulled the ice cream off slowly then swallowed. "Thank you." He accepted another bite before kissing her. His lips, lightly chilled and sweet, lingered on hers before he eased back.

She gazed into his sincere eyes and felt better after their talk. He was definitely stable in every way.

"I guess if you feel Rebar will be an asset to the group, I'll do my best to control my emotions. I'm still angry with him and Chamber."

"Are you coming back out with me or staying in?" he asked. "I can't leave the guys all night. We have matters to discuss, especially what Shook knows. He doesn't have the luxury of time since he's stringing Malika along."

"I'll come. Won't make me look good to sit in here and pout. Besides, I'd like to get better acquainted with the others. I barely got to meet Moss and Levi in Raton."

"That's my girl." He pulled her off the bed and into his arms for another kiss.

By the time they'd meandered back to the fire, she'd finished her ice cream, so she tossed the empty carton into the flames. The guys were lounging about on the ground chatting quietly.

Rush walked over to Chamber. "I need a word with you," he told him.

Chamber pushed to his feet. "Everything okay?"

Without warning, Rush landed a hard right hook to Chamber's jaw, knocking him back down. "I've told you before, don't flirt with rescues. We're all aware of your rep with ladies. That's not what Ricochet does. Your friend can stay. He's on probation. He'll be a probie till further notice."

Chamber rubbed his jaw then gave a relenting nod.

Nobody said a word or seemed the slightest bit bothered by Rush's firm physical reminder. Cameo cast Chamber a pointed look, relieved that Rush had set him straight.

"I'm sorry, Halo. I never meant to lead you on. But I told you the truth about Rebar. I honestly didn't know he was driving down. In fact, during our last phone call, I told him that he'd have serious competition if he tried to get you back."

"I'm not a carnival prize, Chamber. And at the moment, there is no competition. I'm seeing Rush."

He blinked in shock. "Wow. Fast. That explains why I've been decked twice in an hour." He laughed it off. "Serves me right for messing with the wrong woman."

Rebar's expression saddened at her confession. However, he had nobody to blame but himself. He'd dumped her cold and Rush was waiting in the wings. She knew it wasn't cut and dry, that she still had feelings for Rebar and might always love him to some degree. Even so, Rush was right. No matter what Rebar said or did in the future, Cameo would always wonder in her deepest thoughts if he was still in love with her twin. The only reason he sent Camille packing was because she had betrayed him. She could waltz back into his world without notice and lure him right back into her web again.

And Cameo refused to become the volleyball in their game. She realized it was quite possible that Rebar and Camille could still end up together in the end after they'd explored all other avenues. And in the process, who knew how many lives they'd send into chaos? She wasn't about to let them bounce her heart around while they sorted their feelings.

Suddenly, she realized all eyes were on her. Despite her nervousness, she masked her emotions with a smile. "I'm sorry for wasting valuable time. I got blindsided but I'm good now. Please, go on with your meeting. Shook is walking a tenuous line that we need to consider."

Rush didn't even attempt to conceal his pride. "You heard my woman. Let's get down to business." He plopped onto the grass and gently pulled her onto his lap, wrapping both arms around her from behind.

She leaned back against him, resting her head against his shoulder then whispered in his ear. "Just a word, huh?"

He turned his head just far enough that their eyes met. A mischievous grin formed sexy dimples at the corners of his mouth. "I'm not a big talker."

CHAPTER THREE

Cameo listened to their conversation. Rush's comforting arm around her felt so good, so right. She looked at their faces as they talked. The camaraderie between them was palpable. They were a family, brothers in arms . . .

"Malika is perfect bait to keep tabs on the General," Shook told them as they discussed how to best proceed. "She's sweet on me and arrogant. Thinks she's running the show. An interesting twist of fate we didn't see coming."

"How'd you slip away alone?" asked Rush.

"Told her the truth, that I need to meet with my friends if she wants our help. She's waiting for me. Then we're headed to Amarillo."

"Amarillo?" Rush sounded surprised. "What's in Amarillo?"

"Malika seems to think the old man is there. She said something about his second battle station."

"That's only about five hours away. Does anyone know that Ricochet is based here in Dallas?"

"Not that I can think of," Shook replied. "Unless Rebar told Camille where he was headed."

"No," Rebar spoke up. "She doesn't even know I left Colorado. I locked up the house and drove out in the middle of the night. Plus, I'm tracking her, so I know she didn't follow."

"You're tracking Camille? How?" asked Rush.

"*Face Palm,*" Cameo said, then looked at Rebar. "You slipped *Face Palm* onto Camille?"

Rebar nodded. "I didn't want to give away your location.

Like I said, my loyalty is here, with all of you."

"What's *Face Palm*?" Rush looked at Rebar then at her.

Rebar grinned. "Remember how I was able to track Missy and Joan in Raton? I used the same system on Camille. My new invention is now actively in the testing phase. Since it worked once, I figured I'd try it again to see how long it stays in the host."

"I'm impressed. Do you know where she's at right now?"

Rebar pulled a phone from the inner pocket of his leather jacket and studied it for a few minutes. His brow wrinkled curiously. "Strange . . . she's not at Shade's. According to my data, she just crossed into a place called Texline." He looked around the group. "Anyone know where that is?"

"Northwest of Amarillo," Rush replied, visibly connecting the dots. "Seems like Malika has summoned her daughter. Why? What are those two women up to now?" His attention went to Shook. "You're up, buddy. Work your magic. Find out why they're going to powwow in Amarillo."

"Got it," Shook said with a nod.

Cameo didn't understand. "What makes you think they're both meeting there?"

"A hunch," Rush replied. "Shook already confirmed Malika's destination point. There's not much to see in Texline. Just a small border town where they're connecting. Camille is obviously following the route from Colorado Springs to Amarillo."

"Shook best be careful," she warned.

"I agree," Rebar added. "Chamber and I were at the Louisiana takedown. It was pretty obvious that Malika is unpredictable and loyal to nobody but herself."

Rush looked at Chamber. "How many soldiers are running with Shade these days?"

"Last I heard, just Ammo and Bullet. Oh, and Jackson, his most loyal comrade," Chamber told him. "Whatcha thinking?"

"I'm wondering if Camille is alone or if she's gathered her own little troop. Something about this feels . . . can't really put my finger on it. Something's gnawing at my gut."

"Shady?" Cameo scoffed.

Rush laughed. "Yeah. Shady as hell. Ratty."

"When did you slip *Face Palm* onto her?" Cameo asked Rebar.

He glanced at his device. "Forty-eight hours ago. The day I overheard her and Malika scheming in my office, I decided to be proactive instead of waiting to see what they did next. I didn't get close enough to Malika. She bolted right away . . . cagy woman that one. But Camille was easy. While she was trying to work her magic on me, I simply attached it to her back."

Cameo cringed at the thought of him making out with her twin, but she hid her pain. The situation between Ricochet and team Malika had just leveled up and her emotions over a breakup would have to sit on the backburner for now.

"Given that, we may have a few days left to track her then, right?" Rush asked.

Rebar nodded.

"Thanks, man," Rush said. "Your invention just saved us from another potential ambush."

"Glad I could help." Rebar smiled a little.

Cameo could see how much it meant to him to be part of this group. He was lost when she met him and appeared just as lost when he first showed up tonight with Chamber. Her sister had really done a number on the guy. Cameo almost felt sorry for him but reminded herself of how heartlessly he had dropped her for her twin.

"I take it we're going to hang back a bit," Stoke said.

"Yeah." Rush nodded. "I thought we'd be able to ride in and wrap this up rather quickly."

"Nothing is that simple when my mother is involved." Cameo sighed.

"Ah don't feel bad," Rider told her. "We're used to complications. Domestic shit sucks."

Silence fell. Only the loud crackling of the fire disturbed the stillness. Nobody said anything for a little while and Rush rested his chin on her shoulder. Cameo's gaze drifted over the men. They all seemed to be digesting the new information they'd just learned.

She did some deep thinking herself, reflecting on the few conversations she'd had with Malika. Cameo pondered what she knew about Camille along with their tense exchanges over the past few months, and everything Camille had told her about their mother. She barely knew either of them, yet it felt like a lifetime of drama had taken place.

Then suddenly it dawned on her. Malika hadn't changed one bit. She was about to set Ricochet up for a fall in her quest to carry out a forty-year-old vendetta. Men were her enemy. Mere pawns to further her agenda. She didn't care who got hurt.

But why Ricochet? If she's hot for Shook, why would she want to destroy his family? This baffled her. *And what's Camille's role this time?* She hadn't forgotten how her mother had used her sister the first time around.

"Are you okay?" Rush murmured against her ear.

"Yeah. Just have a lot on my mind."

"I think all the guys are backtracking their thoughts right now. Maybe we should take a break, have some fun before Shook has to leave."

"Sounds good to me." She chose not to disclose her thoughts until she had time to mull them over. She didn't want to sound like an alarmist. Besides, these men were experienced and street savvy. She didn't want to insult them or come off as an arrogant know-it-all.

"I'm worried about Shook," she said quietly to Rush.

"What's on your mind, babe?" He gave her a questioning look. "I can tell something's bothering you."

She shrugged. "I don't want to sound paranoid or that I doubt the skills of your family."

"You won't insult us. Talk to me."

"I think it's a setup. I can't shake this feeling that Malika and the General are in cahoots, for lack of a better word. And it wouldn't surprise me if Camille and Shade's troop are on their side."

"That's an interesting take. Why would Malika join forces with her worst enemy?"

"I don't know. I can't quite put it all together that's why I didn't want to say anything."

"Chamber did say that Malika seemed unusually together right after they rescued her," Rush told her. "I never thought much about it until now."

"Nothing makes sense." She sighed in frustration. "Malika sending Camille after Rebar the way she did. Her remarks about me falling right into her plan. It's almost as if she's the puppet master pulling all the strings. But to what purpose? What is she really after?"

His eyes searched hers. She saw concern shadow his face and knew he was beginning to worry even more over her.

"You don't mind if I share your thoughts with Shook, do ya?" he asked in his nonintrusive manner that always set her at ease.

"I don't mind. He shouldn't take her lightly."

"How would you like to hang out with Rider and Stoke while I give Shook a heads up?"

"Worried I'll go wandering with the cows again?" she quipped.

He laughed a little. "Nah. Just thought you'd enjoy getting to know them."

"You're a horrible liar." She feigned a scolding look.

He shrugged and grinned. "That's a good thing then. I'd hate to be a good liar."

She gave him a playful swat but smiled, nonetheless. "I'd love to visit with your friends, especially if it'll ease your mind."

They strolled past Rebar and Chamber who were sitting near the fire with Moss and Levi, casually drinking.

"Taking her to meet the riffraff, eh?" Chamber teased.

"She's already ridden with you four clowns. Time she gets to know the hard crew," Rush shot back.

"Hey!" Levi protested.

Rush laughed and kept walking. "Don't worry, babe. I just like picking on them. Keeps 'em humble."

"And who keeps you humble?"

His gaze met hers. "You."

She didn't have a fitting response to that, so offered none. He had a sharp wit and often surprised her with his blatant remarks. The man was anything but predictable and carried an air of authority, which kept her intrigued.

"Rider, Stoke . . . why don't you tell Halo about yourselves while I go have a chat with Shook."

"Gladly," Stoke replied and scooted over to make a spot for her between them on the ground. "Have a seat, Halo. Need a cold beer?"

"No thanks, I just ate a pint of ice cream. Not sure they'd mix." She smiled politely then plopped onto the grass between the two long-haired roughnecks.

"Don't let her wander off," Rush told them before he walked away.

Cameo watched him grab two cold bottles from the cooler then saunter over to Shook.

"So, Halo, how do you like Texas?" asked Rider. "I heard you grew up in Europe."

"Yes. I spent almost my entire life there until recently.

Texas seems nice. I had a good time in Austin when I first got here."

"Austin's a great place," Stoke chimed in. "Always something to do there. Great food. Fun nightlife."

"Where are you guys from?" she asked.

"We live here in Dallas," Rider said. "Along with the others, except Chamber and Hunter, who have yet to settle in one place."

"I can kind of relate to that. Since my arrival in the States back in May I've been in Colorado, New Mexico, and here. Not much in the way of variety, with the exception of Austin. Beautiful city with lots of activity."

"Stick with us, Halo. We'll show you all fifty states," Stoke said with a smile. "We love to ride. Are you a biker babe?"

"Um . . . not really." She laughed lightly. "My very first ride was with Rush down to Raton."

"What'd you think of riding on the back of his Harley?"

"It was exhilarating. I wish it had ended better . . ." Her thoughts drifted.

Stoke's expression shifted to that of compassion. "Yeah. I heard about the crash. You were both lucky to walk away."

"I'd say *limped* is more the word." She scoffed. "Well, technically we were dragged off the road like animals."

"You're one tough mama to save Rush like you did," Stoke said.

Rider nodded in agreement. "And after taking a beating yet. Where'd a sweet little thing like you learn such survival skills?"

"I think it's inborn. I've been fighting my way through life since I was a child. It never occurred to me not to fight. And saving Rush just came naturally. He was so brave. I owed him the same. He took a bullet trying to save my mother who ended up betraying the very men who risked their lives to help her."

Rider studied her face then said, "Rush told us about the angel. That had to be something incredible."

Her thoughts whipped back to that little girl, then to the hot chemistry between her and Rush. "Yeah . . . incredible." She shrugged off a chill to stop herself from spiraling. "Enough about me. What do you guys do when you're not riding with Ricochet."

"Work," Rider replied, his entrancing eyes clearly searching her thoughts.

"Girlfriends? Wives?" she pried.

"Sometimes." Stoke laughed. "No wives. Seems marriage doesn't mix well with what we do."

"Where do you work?"

"We're business partners," Rider told her. "We own a construction company."

"That sounds interesting. What do you build? Houses?"

"More like bridges, tunnels, railroad, energy plants . . . stuff like that. Heavy construction."

"Oh." She looked them over and could picture them doing such work. A vast difference from what her job entailed.

"Do you work?" Stoke asked.

"I have a career. I traveled around Europe, South Africa and Australia for it. I haven't found work here yet. I'm hoping to land a forestry position around Austin. But Rush wants me to stay here until I'm feeling more settled."

"You do sound like a rolling stone." Rider chuckled. "What did you do in all those places?"

"Worked with wildlife, mostly endangered species. Fought against poachers. Studied climate change and ways to help the environment. Nature is a delicate balance."

"Saving the world one elephant at a time, huh?" Stoke smiled.

"Something like that."

"A noble calling," he added, much to her relief. "I hope you don't think less of us for being on the opposite end of the spectrum."

"Opposite? Are you guys trophy hunters?" she asked him bluntly, then realized she probably sounded rude. "I'm sorry. That came out wrong." She felt herself slipping into that dark void again. The mention of trophies reminded her of another man — a beast.

Stoke furrowed his brows in a scowl. "I know we're a bit rough, but do we look that bad?"

"Sorry." She toyed with a lock of her hair, suddenly nervous. "I didn't mean to be so direct."

"It's cool," Rider said with a wink. "You're upfront. I like it." He paused and gazed at her, then added, "No, we don't hunt. Actually, our company goes above and beyond to preserve wildlife habitats when a new project comes up."

"Yeah, don't let Rider's vampire appearance fool you," Stoke chortled. "He's just a big softy inside when it comes to animals."

"I'm relieved to hear that. We could not be friends if you were trophy hunters."

Rider arched his brows. "Wow . . . that's harsh . . . and a bit judgy."

"Sorry but I have my reasons. I abhor anyone who kills for sport and then proudly display their kills on a wall."

"You definitely speak your mind," he countered sharply.

"I have my reasons. My fa —" She stopped short. "The General. I guess . . . I'm not even sure he *is* my father. But that's another story." Her gut tightened. "I'm gonna grab one of those beers after all," she told them then pushed to her feet and walked away.

Flashbacks of the General's house hit without warning. She grabbed a cold brew and kept on walking down toward the lower pasture. Glancing back, she saw them conversing with puzzled expressions. Before they could realize she had not returned, she vanished from their view behind a cluster of trees.

Crouching down, Cameo pressed the cold bottle to her face. The cooling sensation felt pleasing. She closed her eyes and tried to clear her head. Thunder rumbled in the distance. Something cracked up above and she cringed. A twig dropped, scraping her bare arm. It caused the memories to return in full force.

"I'll give you something to cry about."

His threat reverberated around her. She clapped both hands over her ears and tucked her chin to her chest.

"Pretty little girls are nothing but trouble," he growled. "Get over here, child."

Crack! The sound of his whip smacking the wall made her cringe.

Run! She told herself. Run now! She sprang to her feet and bolted down the sloping hill.

"Cameo! Don't run from me, girl. You'll only make it worse. Papa needs to keep his girls in line. Your mother never wanted you. She left. Do you see her around? No. She left me stuck with your scrawny little ass to raise. But don't you worry, I'll get her one day. Malika will pay for her crimes. Now where are you, child?"

She never slowed until she found herself knee-deep in water. Face down she went into the lake, submerging herself in the dark water to hide from his wrath. She was an excellent swimmer for her age and could hold her breath underwater longer than any kid in her class.

Lying on her back, she let her face crest the water for air for a moment but tried not to move for fear of him spotting her. Suddenly, she heard people, voices. They were talking amongst themselves, seemingly worried about something.

"Halo!" a muffled male voice called with a sense of urgency. "Halo, where are you, babe?" He sounded panicked. "Dear God, please help me find her," she heard him mutter.

"How'd she slip away?" the first man asked.

"In the blink of an eye. We were talking, she said she needed a drink and then she was just gone," another replied.

"What the hell about? What'd you say to her?"

"Nothing really. Our jobs, animals. She asked if we were trophy hunters and then her mood just kinda plummeted."

"PTSD attack," the man who called her Halo replied.

"Has she done this before?" a third man asked.

"Last night. She took off while I was in the shower. I have no idea where she went but she returned all scratched up. We joked about her roaming with the cows."

"She's hiding from him."

"Who?"

"The General. We need to coax her out. Assure her she's safe."

"All of us, or just one of us?"

"She's cagy as hell. Send the *hunters* away . . . and Chamber. She no longer trusts him."

"She doesn't trust you either, Rebar," one of them growled.

"You want me to help you or not?"

"Everyone, go to the house, except Rebar. We'll find her and be back soon," the first man said.

Cameo slithered through the water silently to shore, then crawled into the bushes. Her mind reeled. She racked her brain for reason. *Where am I? Who are they? They know the General. Are they his friends? Are they helping him track me?* She trembled beneath the weight of her uncontrollable memories.

"Halo, please, baby, don't hide. You're worrying me," the first man pleaded while walking around the field.

She peeked through a couple branches and saw two men, who bore a strong resemblance to one another, searching for her. Could she trust them? A shiver trickled up her spine. *Halo. Why is he calling me Halo?*

"Cameo, it's me, Rebar. Don't be afraid. We're on your side. Remember our peaceful nights binging on Ramen and talking about our cars?"

Her stomach growled with hunger at the mention of her favorite noodles. This man knew her. He felt familiar. Slowly her disturbed thoughts calmed as she pondered his words. Then as quickly as it had attacked, the nightmare vanished. She looked around, then down at herself and saw what a mess she was, covered in dirt and briars.

Sheepishly, she crawled from the brush and pushed to her feet. "I'm over here," she said weakly.

They hurried toward her, then slowed and approached in a calm manner. She threw her arms around Rebar and buried her face against his neck. His familiar scent of leather and fine cologne greeted her. Her mind still felt somewhat muddled, like a hangover.

Rebar hugged her fiercely, as if they hadn't embraced for a very long time. "I'm sorry the PTSD got you, too, kitten," he murmured. "I never thought you, of all people, would have to suffer like this. But I can help you through it, Camille."

She recoiled as if he'd thrown acid on her. His inability to separate her from Camille cut like a knife.

His eyes widened with sudden regret. "I'm sorry! I didn't mean to—"

She cut him off by delivering a rebuking slap to his face and turned away. Her mind was crystal clear again. She focused on Rush who stood by with a pained expression on his face. Tears sprang to her eyes. She didn't know what to say so she sprinted up the hill with every intention of hopping into her car and speeding away from this hell.

Rush chased and caught her, wrapped his long, muscled arms around her and tackled her to the ground. She burst into sobs.

"Please . . . let me . . . go. I'm a mess. I want . . . to go . . . home," she cried.

He pulled her up to his chest and held her close, tenderly

stroking her hair. "You are home, angel. You just don't know it yet."

CHAPTER FOUR

"I'm sorry I ruined the evening," Cameo said to the group of men lounging about Rush's living room. A fierce gale rattled the windows and rain slashed against the glass. There was a sudden chill in the house, so Rush started a fire in the fireplace. The flames sent cozy reflections over the walls.

"Ah no worries, Halo. We were about to get driven in by the storm anyway. You saved us from getting drenched," Rider told her. "We're the ones who owe you an apology, well . . . I do anyway for the way I spoke to you. I'm very sorry, babe."

"It's okay." She pulled a soft blanket from the loveseat and draped it around herself. She still felt chilled from the unexpected flashback.

Stoke gave Rider a hard nudge. "You'll have to excuse my wingman. He doesn't have a deft touch with words like some of us do."

Rider rolled his eyes and scoffed. "He's right. I have no excuse."

"I'm not always great with words either." She offered him a warm smile.

"Now that we know you're struggling, we'll watch for triggers," Stoke assured her.

"This time it was actually a breaking twig that triggered it but thank you all for being so understanding." She looked up at Rush who sat with an arm caringly around her. "Especially you. I don't imagine it was easy for you to see all that."

"I'm strong enough to bend. We discussed this so don't

worry your pretty little self over it." He placed a short yet affectionate kiss on her lips. "This is one of those emotional times I mentioned during our night in Austin."

She remembered that night clearly. He'd swept her off her feet on the dance floor then they laid awake talking for hours after. His inner strength was as impressive as his outward brawn.

Cameo noticed Rebar appeared severely out of sorts. She didn't feel sorry for him, though perhaps she should. Her feelings toward him confused her. For a few moments, he'd felt like the most familiar safe thing in her world then without warning, *slam!* Camille was back in her face. This was the invisible wall Rush had seen between them from the beginning—the barrier Cameo tried to ignore until it broke her.

"Hey guys . . . and Halo," said Shook. "I better take off. I don't wanna leave Malika alone for too long. She may get restless and take off. We can't lose our link to the General now. We've waited too long, rescued so many victims from his trafficking ring. This time he's not getting off the hook."

Rush gave a nod. "Remember what I told you. Malika may not be the only bait in this operation."

"I hear ya." Shook's attention went to Cameo. "Hang in there, girl. We'll get through this thing yet."

"Be safe, Shook. Seriously, don't underestimate her," she said. "My mother is unpredictably dangerous."

"Don't worry. I won't. I've been briefed on her history." He flashed a disarming smile, then took his leave.

Cameo liked him and easily saw why Rush had chosen Shook as his wingman. They appeared extremely compatible and streetwise.

"What's the plan now, Rush?" asked Levi.

"We should send a couple scouts up to Amarillo. Who wants to go? I don't want anyone making a move. Just ride up and see if you can pinpoint Camille's location. I'm guessing it will lead to the General or Malika or preferably both."

"Levi and I can ride up," Moss volunteered. "If we leave now, we'll be there by sunup. No sense wasting time since we don't know how long Rebar can track her."

Rush turned toward Rebar. "You still onboard with us? I get that this is an awkward situation. If you want to bow out, not one of us will blame you."

"No," Rebar said with a shake of his head. "I deserve Cameo's wrath. I pledged my loyalty to you guys. I meant it . . . that is if Cam . . . Halo will accept my presence and my apology."

Again, all eyes were on her. She squirmed inside but forced a faint smile. "You need a better family than the one you had. I never want to be the reason you go back to living alone," she told him. "If you've found your place here with Ricochet, then I'll work on forgiving you. I know Chamber's your best friend. I'd never do anything to cause you pain . . . no matter what."

"Now that's class," Stoke said, lifting his bottle in salute.

Rider did the same. "Indeed."

Chamber nodded in agreement, then said, "How about Rebar and I ride up with Moss and Levi? Wouldn't hurt to have a few more bodies up there watching out for each other. Besides, Rebar's got the tracking on Camille. We should put him closer to her so she doesn't slip out of range."

Rush thought for a moment then agreed. "Yeah. Be discreet, though. Camille has seen all four of you."

"We're the soul of discretion," Chamber said with a grin.

Cameo had a feeling Chamber was smoothly diffusing the tension between her and Rebar, and possibly even himself. She didn't imagine Chamber enjoyed getting belted twice earlier. Served him right for playing both sides. He'd had every intention of hitting on her even if he denied it.

Rush waved Moss over to them. "Keep a close eye on those

two. Remember, the new guy is on probation. If he shows a hint of softening toward Camille or even her mother, get him out of the way. Got it?"

"Yep. Don't worry, man. I'll take care of things. Nobody's getting burnt this time. Gotta admit, the new guy's tracking will come in handy."

"Yeah. And if he stays on course, he'll be a valuable addition to our family," Rush said. "But until we're sure of his loyalty, we need to be alert."

"I agree. The four of us are crashing at my place until this is over. I'll see you tomorrow." Moss bid them farewell, gestured for Levi to come, then left. Chamber and Rebar followed.

Rider and Stoke moved to a sofa adjacent to them. "Good move letting Chamber and Rebar ride up with them," Stoke said.

"It was Chamber's idea." Rush shrugged. "No doubt, he wanted a break from us tonight."

"My presence has created too much drama." Cameo sighed.

"Nah," Stoke refuted. "Not the first time we've had to sort the pecking order. Chamber crossed the line. Now he's gotta reconcile with his actions. It'll do him good to pair with Rebar. They've known each other for years."

"I appreciate your casual take on things. It's been a crazy night for me. I'm not used to all this tension. My life was calm before Malika walked into it."

"We thrive on the chase," Rider added. "Don't stress over these things."

"Thanks." She smiled gratefully.

"I assume the two of you are crashing here tonight," Rush said.

"Yeah. I've had a few too many to ride and if we're to get an early start, we'll take one of your guest rooms or bunk out here on the floor," Stoke replied.

"Take a room. No need to sleep on the floor." Rush stood and took Cameo's hand. "We should all get some sleep."

Rush led her to his master bedroom after they said goodnight to Rider and Stoke, the only two bunking with them.

She said a silent prayer for Shook, that God would watch over him as he ventured out alone with Malika. She also prayed for the entire Ricochet family, for their safety and success in apprehending a dangerous criminal—or two.

"Well, hello, gorgeous," Malika said in greeting when Shook walked into their hotel room. "I was beginning to wonder if you were coming back." She lay across the king bed, wearing a sheer red negligee slit up to her hip. One of her shapely long legs was posed invitingly over the sheets.

"Sorry to keep you waiting." He tossed his jacket on a chair. "You look stunning."

"I'm glad you approve." A mischievous grin curved her painted red lips. She'd loosened her long sleek black hair from its braid and fanned it around her shoulders. "Now come on over here and give me what I need."

He strolled to the edge of the bed and let her undo his jeans as he peeled off his shirt. "I should shower first," he muttered.

"No need," she murmured. Her hair brushed his abs and her nails dug into his lower back. "I've waited long enough."

He sucked in a sharp breath, hating himself for enjoying her sexual aggression while knowing they were enemies. Nevertheless, she'd targeted him the moment he rescued her in Raton, and she hadn't given any signs of backing down. Whatever she wanted, whatever she demanded—he gave. And as pleasurable as it felt, their trysts left him feeling sullied.

After she'd taken her fill of him orally, she pulled him onto the bed to slake her own lust using his body. When she finished, she rolled onto her back, a satisfied smile on her face.

"Are we still driving to Amarillo in the morning?" she asked without even a glance his way.

"Yeah. That's what you want, right?"

"Yes, my love. Tomorrow the General will face his past. Are your friends still helping us?"

"I said they would. We don't go back on our word. Have I given you reason for doubt?" He looked over at her.

"None," she replied, finally turning those seductive black eyes on him. "You've been a perfect stud since the day I hopped onto the back of your motorcycle. And now, you've convinced your friends to help me. I will reward you handsomely."

"I don't expect anything. There are no strings attached." He raked a hand through his hair and sighed. "Some people are givers."

She laughed sardonically. "Yes. And you surely know how to give a woman what she needs." She let one finger glide down his chest to his navel. "I'm glad I snapped you up before one of my feisty daughters had a chance."

"Seems to me both your daughters are taken."

"Mm-hm. Shade laid claim to Camille and Rebar chased after Cameo but lost out to Rush."

"Rebar tossed her away at a very bad time. He could've handled it better."

"Perhaps. Either way, Cameo isn't good enough for a Damocles man. She's too soft. Allows her heart to govern her actions." Malika gave a slight eyeroll. "I've never really been impressed by her, gallivanting around the world, saving animals. Now Camille . . . highly educated Registered Nurse, skilled in healing people, that's worth something."

Shook remained outwardly emotionless so she couldn't see how appalled he felt. "Is that why Cameo was sent away?"

"I had nothing to do with that. The General shipped her off when he married and adopted those two dimwitted daughters. His wife didn't like Cameo around because she was so much prettier than Missy and Joan."

"Adopted?" Shook arched both brows.

"Yes. He can't father children. But nobody else knows that. He kept his secret well-hidden like men of his stature would do." Disdain hung on her voice.

Shook realized this woman was a closet of secrets. Cameo had unduly suffered because of the lies told to her all her life. He lay quietly, knowing that most women loved to talk and given the chance would inadvertently disclose things they'd kept buried deep within, especially to a lover's attentive ear.

Malika rolled onto her side facing him. She traced the contours of his chest. "Do you work out?"

"A little."

"You are a fine specimen of male flesh for your age." Her fingers floated up and down his torso.

"Thanks. You're not so bad yourself." He mustered a smile and a wink to keep her in this yielding state of mind.

"And a good listener. Most men fall asleep after I'm done. Not you. Strong, virile. My, my, I've found quite a treasure in you, dear Shook."

He accepted her kiss then stared into eyes that shone with mystery. He wanted her to continue talking so he lay quietly and let her hands roam as she pleased.

"Did they tell you how the General and I met?" she asked.

"No. I've only met your daughter and Rebar two brief times."

"I see. Well, Cameo is good at keeping secrets, I'll give her that. I'll give you the short version." She scoffed while continuing the teasing caresses as if to keep him in a state of arousal to cloud his mind. "I was unofficially betrothed to Congressman Jared Connor when his best friend, the General, decided he wanted me. Being that the General had powerful connections that Jared utilized in his climb up the political ladder, he used those favors to bully Jared into sharing me."

"I'm sorry to hear that." Shook folded both arms behind his head and forced himself to ignore her potent physical and toxic allure.

"When I ended up pregnant, those two men took me into hiding. After all, they didn't want anyone to know they'd impregnated a poor Native American girl from the rez."

"You're Native American?"

"Full-blooded Lakota," she replied. "Can't you tell?"

"Wow. I didn't know. That explains your exquisite beauty."

She smiled up at him. "Sweet talker."

"Just the truth. Something tells me that you already know how beautiful you are."

"Ah, and insightful, too." She laughed a little. "Anyway, they took me to some military housing. The General kept me locked up until the girls were born. He and I both knew that Jared was the father but I agreed to the lie in exchange for freedom. I was involved with organizations the General found offensive. He had me cornered."

"Yet, you let Cameo believe he was her father?"

"I had no choice. He called all the shots from the day he caught Jared and me in bed. The General switched the paternity test to make it appear that each twin had a different father. He dictated how the girls would be raised. Jared got Camille and he took Cameo. And that's what I want to know, is *why* he did that."

"That's why you've been tracking the man? To find out why he kept a daughter that wasn't his, then sent her away?" Shook was shocked and wondered if he could even believe this woman.

"Part of it," she replied. "And to make him pay for

torturing me and Cameo. Though I don't like Cameo as much as I do Camille, I was heartbroken to hear what that man put her through. Everyone thinks I'm cold. Perhaps I am. But they can't judge me until they've put on my boots and walked my road."

"Cameo is amazing. How can you favor one over the other?"

Malika shrugged with indifference. "She's just different. She's not like Camille and me. Camille can bend a man to her will at any given moment. She won the heart of bigtime oil man Shade and his millionaire half-brother Rebar in a month's time. I put it to the test that day in Rebar's home. I goaded Camille into pursuing Rebar to see if she could steal the man right out from under her sister. And she did just that. No man can resist Camille. No man can resist me."

Shook's mind reeled. This woman had methods of operation that blew him away.

"Now the time of reckoning is at hand," she continued in her soft, sultry voice. "The General will be forced to answer that burning question I've carried all these years. And it's time the girls knew the truth about their paternity, don't you think?" She gazed up at him.

He looked down at her face. "That's why we're going to Amarillo?"

"Yes. With you and Ricochet at my side, the General can't hurt me. He'll be outnumbered. I had a driver take me to his home in Santa Fe because I wanted answers. I was blindsided by Joan and Missy. I didn't know they'd faked Joan's death. My plan didn't work out the first time. When Cameo showed up, posing as Camille, the General had taken me into hiding at Raton. I knew Cameo wouldn't give up. She's too loyal that way. I knew she'd find help and rescue me."

"For a woman who says she doesn't like her daughter, you sure put a lot of faith in her."

Malika let out a short laugh. "Camille would've let me rot. She's stubborn and proud like her mother. Not sweet Cameo. She can't hold a grudge against anyone. That's why I tracked her down . . . to assist in my mission. Once I met her, I knew she'd fall right into place and be instrumental in drawing her twin out. Camille didn't budge on reconciling with me until you and I showed up and said Rebar was hurt. She sure came running then, didn't she?"

"You played them?" He tried to hide his disgust.

"Of course. Camille was being a petulant brat. I knew how to light a fire under her and get Shade to go along with it."

"Wow. I must admit. I'm shocked."

"Desperate women do crazy things, Shook. Don't ever forget that."

"Don't worry. I won't forget." He committed everything she said to memory. "I'm curious. Didn't Jared question the paternity? After all, different fathers to identical twins is unheard of. Surely, a man of his intelligence knew that."

"He knew the truth, knew that his comrade was sterile from a war injury. However, by then the General owned him. We managed to keep Jared quiet until he got old and developed a conscience. He started making noise about telling the girls he was their father. He wanted to include Cameo in his will. He wanted to meet her . . . his other twin daughter."

"Whoa. Heavy secrets to bear for forty years."

"Everyone has family skeletons, Shook. Don't act so surprised."

He was taken back by her sudden shift in demeanor, yet she remained cool. "Yeah . . . guess so. I've seen a lot."

"I know that you have," she said. "And I know the purpose of Ricochet and the oath they hold dear. That's why I can finally, after all these years, tell someone everything. You must keep my confidence because you rescued me."

Wow, he thought. *She doesn't miss a beat. Cameo was right to warn me. This female is dangerous.* "You're right."

"You see, darling. The General doesn't want me dead. He wants me in his bed. But I abhor the man. Therein lies the conflict. We did, however, agree on one thing . . . the need to hush Jared for good. Jared was about to change his will and split everything down the middle between the two girls. We couldn't have that. We didn't want anyone to know the paternity secret. The last thing we needed was a scandal that would draw attention to our . . . affiliations. I never wanted my daughters to know *all* the dirt. But none of that matters now."

"I read that the congressman committed suicide," Shook said, recalling the news headlines from a year ago.

Again, she laughed. "He had help. We put the man out of his misery. He was about to blow four worlds apart. That was simply unacceptable. The General and I created a special lethal cocktail for our dear old friend, Jared. One of the General's men slipped it into Jared's regular bottle of bourbon, and just like that, our secret was safe forever."

"You killed him?"

"If you want to see it that way. Just like I killed Dale. I did all involved a favor. Shade and Rebar's half-brother was a pathetic excuse of a man, so when I dropped him, I do believe Shade was relieved. And when I helped the General put together a special drink for Jared, I did *everyone* a favor. Nobody in his family, or mine, needed that kind of drama to go public. But did he show any gratitude for my help? No. The man acts like he can do everything without aid. It was my contacts that obtained the undetectable chemicals needed to escort Jared from this world."

"Glad I'm on your good side." He managed a wan smile.

"As am I," she said. "I promised to lead you to the General and I'll keep that promise. All I ask in return is that you protect me from him."

Shook struggled to process her level of lethality. He'd

never been the nervous type, but tonight apprehension crept over him like icicles put there by the icy fingers touching him at this very moment.

"Don't worry, lover," she purred, switching from femme fatale to kitten again. "You're in no danger. I'd never destroy such a fine hunk of man." She straddled his waist. "Now how about relieving some of my tension. I get so stressed talking about that evil beast."

At this point, Shook wasn't confident he could meet her expectations. His libido was strong, but he also had a heart. Regardless, she managed to get her way with an almost supernatural touch that made his body defy his mind. He cursed the treacherous lust she'd induced.

In a few hours, they'd be on their way to Amarillo. Malika had cleverly orchestrated a grand finale to her self-seeking agenda. He lay there, eyes closed, while she had her way with him.

His thoughts went to Cameo and Camille, two daughters betrayed forty years ago, walking into an emotional ambush. He had no choice but to let the family scene play out as it would. He couldn't discern whether Camille was a victim or a player, as she had seemed fully reconciled with her mother.

His heart went out to Cameo—the unfavored daughter cast aside, then lured back to play her part in a game that might surely find her on the losing end. Cameo's situation was the reason Ricochet did what they did.

The woman feeding her insatiable lust on his body right now believed she had all her chess pieces perfectly in place. But what she didn't know was that she'd overlooked a crucial factor in her scheme—Ricochet's secret weapon.

She'd just confessed to murdering two men in cold blood to an undercover FBI Agent.

Except, he had no proof . . .

Not yet . . .

CHAPTER FIVE

A*marillo.* Cameo gazed at the sky. She'd traveled up and down tornado alley several times now since she left Denver. Fortunately, she'd not encountered any twisters but by the looks of today's sky, she wondered. Hot, hazy, and heavy, with the scent of rain hanging strong on the air.

She laid her head against Rush's back as they rumbled through city streets to a rendezvous point with Shook, and supposedly Malika. They hadn't heard otherwise so she assumed her mother was still hanging with Rush's wingman.

Moss had texted them regularly with updates. Camille had not yet been spotted but Rebar still had her on tracking.

They'd been on the road about six hours, not including a few rest stops. She guessed by the position of the sun the time was around noon as the sun perched high overhead and burnt down on her. She felt sweaty beneath her too big leather jacket and helmet that Rush had insisted she wear for safety.

Rush geared down and pulled his Harley into the lot of a small barbeque restaurant. She swore everything in Texas was smothered in sauce.

Moss and Levi were parked beneath the only tree in the area. Rebar and Chamber sat in Rebar's car beside them. Rush eased his bike up beside the four men.

"Any sign of Shook yet?" Rush asked.

"Not yet," Moss replied.

Rush held one hand above his brow to shield the sun and looked at Rebar. "What's tracking show?"

Rebar handed Rush his phone. "Camille's been at this

location since early this morning. I'm assuming she found a hotel during the night."

"That's no hotel," Rush said. "It's a private residence. We'll wait here for Shook." He gave the phone back. "Good work."

They sat in the blistering heat, drinking water to stay hydrated. She declined the offer of food from the restaurant. She didn't think spicy beef would go down well today. She didn't have much of an appetite anyway. They were about to embark into the unknown with people she never wanted to see again. Her only consolation was that Ricochet was with her this time.

And all the guys were heavily packed.

About an hour after their arrival, a man she didn't recognize, driving a magnificent Harley, pulled into the lot. He was dressed in a black tee, black pants, and combat boots. His long hair looked freshly washed and still a bit damp, hanging in unruly strands around his face that was painted strangely. A female passenger was cuddled up behind him. The only thing that made her realize it was Shook, was his passenger.

Malika.

Cameo inwardly cringed. Seeing her mother again forced a swarm of confusing emotions to roil through her. She fought to squash them. Between the heat, the sweat, and the dust, seeing Malika seemed to fit in some weird way.

"Why is Shook wearing face paint?" Cameo whispered to Rush.

"I'll explain later, doll. Just trust me. He's not a freak." Rush softly chuckled.

"I trust you." She discreetly stared at Shook.

His entire face was coated in white makeup. Black lipstick covered his lips and extended into lines from the corners upward to his cheekbones. He'd drawn black face paint around his eyes and again, extended lines vertically running from the upper and lower eyelids. He resembled a scary clown but without color.

51

His appearance was frightening and intimidating. She wondered how her mother felt about his unusual look. Malika was immaculate as always. Not a braided hair was out of place, nor a smudge of her perfectly applied makeup. She wore leather pants, jacket, and knee-high riding boots.

Strangely, they looked good together. With her jet-black hair and his shadowy guise, they radiated force.

"Hello, darling," Malika said in greeting to Cameo. "I'm so relieved to see you've moved on. And as always, you have impeccable taste."

"Hello, Malika. I'm glad to see you're safe. We were concerned that you might try to face the General alone again."

"So sweet of you to care," she countered with a disarming smile. "I learned from my first mistake. I underestimated the man. Now . . . we have help, dear girl, and he will be out of our lives for good."

"Do you know where he's at?" Cameo asked.

"Of course. Nobody knows that man's secrets as I do." She rattled off a street address.

Cameo glanced at Rebar who gave Rush a nod, indicating that it was the same address they'd tracked Camille to. But Malika didn't know that. She didn't know that Ricochet was a step ahead of her. Cameo wondered why Malika had invited Camille to a meeting that had nothing to do with her.

Rush fired up his Harley then said, "Lead the way, Shook."

Shook led out. Rush fell in behind him. Moss and Levi covered their backs with Rebar and Chamber bringing up the rear in Rebar's car.

Cameo hadn't seen Stoke or Rider anywhere this morning. They had left before she and Rush rode out, and so far, no one had mentioned them. She figured they knew what they were doing. Maybe they didn't want Malika to see them. After all, she'd already seen these men in Raton but Rider and Stoke hadn't been part of that run. None of them trusted that Malika was actually the victim here. If she tipped off the General that more men were enroute, he might call in Shade's troop.

Not that Cameo doubted Ricochet's skills. She was merely praying for a quick and nonviolent mission this time. Hopefully, her mother wanted the same but that was like hoping Santa Claus was real. She sighed and clung to Rush as they sped down an interstate.

The blazing sun had dipped toward the west by the time they reached their destination. Ricochet pulled off the road into an abandoned parking lot.

Rush did a visual scan of the area. "Your General likes remote areas," he said with slight sarcasm. "This is a ghost town."

Malika nodded. "He owns all the land around here." She pointed to a metal building. "That used to be a military bunkhouse. It's where he kept me hidden." She motioned toward a row of rundown housing. "Those homes were for his soldiers and where he kept the girls."

A shiver crept through Cameo. She could only imagine what took place in those prisons.

"We'll walk from here," Rush said. He scanned the highway again, as if looking for someone. "Let's go."

Cameo thought for sure her mother would grumble about walking, but to her surprise, Malika strutted alongside Shook with her head held high and no complaints.

They didn't have to walk far before she gestured toward the only well-maintained house on the road. And if the mansion standing out like a beacon wasn't clue enough, Camille's white Shelby in the paved drive confirmed any lingering doubt.

Cameo's twin had driven down from Colorado Springs to Amarillo and was already at the General's secret estate. The only way Camille could've known about this was if Malika had told her. Cameo struggled to grasp why her mother wanted her sister here for this when Camille had no connections to the man.

"Go in as planned," Rush told her.

"I want to take Cameo in with me," she said.

Rush shook his head once. "No."

"Then we have no deal," Malika shot back. "I won't help you bring him down unless I can take my daughter in. This is the day of reckoning for me and my girls. You cannot deny me. I've waited forty years."

The guys exchanged worried looks. She saw apprehension line their faces. Here they were, at the General's most secret domain. They'd have never found it if not for Malika and Camille. This was his nest, the place he'd committed heinous crimes, and then retreated to his lavish home in Santa Fe. This might be their only chance to get him before he slipped away again.

"I'll go," Cameo said.

A pained expression swept through Shook's eyes. "It's too dangerous. I can't let you go up against him again."

Cameo kept her voice low. "All the guys are here, well . . . except Rider and Stoke. If I get into trouble, I know you'll storm the *Bastille* to save me," she kidded a little, to lighten his fear — and her own.

She caught Shook staring at her and the sinking feeling that he knew more than the rest slithered over her.

"I'll be okay. I won't trip out. I'll hold it together. Do you trust me?"

"Yeah. Of course I do. I saw you fight, felt the way you cared for me. But you've been struggling."

"I trust you and Ricochet to keep me safe. I *have* to do this. It may be our only chance to bring him down."

He kissed her lips, softly, affectionately. She felt the love in his kiss and the worry.

"You're the most courageous woman I've met." He kissed

54

her once more.

Malika spoke up. "If you're worried about her safety, let Shook come in with me. I promised I'd lead him to the General in exchange for Ricochet's protection."

"Won't the General be upset to see you with another man?" Rush asked.

"All the better," she responded with a grin.

"I'll watch out for them," Shook said.

Rush gave a relenting nod. "We'll give you fifteen minutes to say what you need to say. Then we're coming in."

"Fair enough." Malika winked at Rush. "Don't worry, darling, your new girlfriend will not be harmed this time."

Malika looped her arm through Shook's. "Are you coming, Cameo?"

"Yes." She followed them toward the house as Rush, Moss, Levi, Chamber, and Rebar scattered around the perimeter. Still no sign of the other two but she trusted Rush's leadership.

There was no knocking at the door this time. Malika had a key. She unlocked the heavy deadbolt and turned the knob, then pushed the door open. Shook glanced around the outside before ushering Cameo in behind her mother.

She didn't feel as nervous as she'd expected upon walking into the man's domain. Perhaps having a force of strong men with her helped. She'd never needed to depend on anyone for anything. Lately, she felt much less independent.

A man's gruff voice sounding from upstairs jarred her to attention.

"You again? Come back for another beating?"

Cameo wondered who he was barking at. Malika hurried down a hallway then up a flight of steps to the second floor. Shook was close behind. He took hold of Cameo's hand and shielded her with his body. They crested the steps and rushed two doors down another hall.

Cameo gasped at the sound of a whip cracking. She pushed past Malika and Shook into the room. Before her stood the General, dressed in full military fatigues with whip in hand, prepared to strike her twin. A mirror image flashed through her mind.

"Wrong daughter, old man!" Cameo snarled upon entering his space. Her arm shot out and deflected a blow meant for Camille, who crouched near the floor. She looked terrified but not injured. Her clothes were still fully intact.

"Are you okay?' she asked Camille.

Camille nodded furiously. "Your timing couldn't be better. He likes to toy with and torment his prey before striking."

He spun toward her, gray eyes blazing with fury. "What the — ?"

She snatched the leather whip straight from his hand with a hard tug and drew her arm back. "Your days of tyranny are over!" And in a move that stunned her, she lashed that braided whip across his pocked face. "I should drop you where you stand."

"Cameo!" cried Malika. "Please, not yet."

Something had changed. Her fear was gone and in its place — a feeling she didn't recognize. Was it rage? Hate? She'd always been passive. While keeping the old man in check with the poised whip, she glanced at her mother. "You have a brief window to disclose why you brought us all here."

"To tell the truth. I've longed for both my girls to hear the cold facts but it had to be like this. It had to be in front of *him*, so he could not deny it or make me a liar." And for once, Malika sounded authentic.

Camille picked herself up off the floor and scooted behind Malika. Her gaze darted around the room from one person to another. She appeared utterly dazed and confused.

"Please," Malika pleaded. "I need answers from him first. I've waited forty years for this day."

"Get on with it then," Cameo said in a tone that sounded like someone else was talking. *When did I become so brave?*

Malika stepped forward but not too close to the man. Then she stopped abruptly and turned toward the door that creaked open. In walked Missy, rifle in hand. The pinkish-haired girl didn't see Shook standing at the door. He grabbed the rifle and shoved her down.

"I suggest you stay there if you know what's good for you," Shook told her with no ado.

Missy took one look around and nodded but didn't say a word.

"Where's the other one?" asked Malika, worry creased her pretty face for the first time since they'd met.

"Were you not listening at Rebar's that day during our quaint little lunch date?" Cameo snapped her fingers at her. "You remember, the one where Rebar dumped me for my sister?"

Malika seemed uncharacteristically frazzled. "Oh . . . that's right. I was distracted. You killed her."

Cameo scoffed. "Yeah . . . I guess so, distracted with your scheme to get Camille and Rebar together."

"You?" Missy scowled from the floor. "*You* killed my sister? I thought that biker dude did it."

"Desperate women do desperate things," Cameo retorted sharply, then glanced at Malika. "Don't they, Mother?"

"Y-yes . . . indeed they do . . ." She stared at Cameo in visible disbelief.

"What the hell is going on here?" the General bellowed. "And who's the freak wearing face paint? Another boytoy, Malika?"

"*Shut up!*" Cameo and Malika shouted back at him at the same time. Then they shot each other a quirky look.

"May I talk now?" Malika asked in a curt tone.

Cameo made a sweeping gesture with her free hand but

kept the whip ready in the other. "The floor's all yours."

Shook had Missy subdued and guarded. Camille shrunk back in visible horror.

Malika turned narrowed eyes on the General. "I've waited forty years for this day. We did everything your way since the day you found me with Jared. What I want to know is *why*? Why you took Cameo if you didn't want her?"

The General's face contorted into a grotesque grimace. His jaw twitched and his eyes transformed into tiny slits. "I never said I didn't want her. I took her so I could have a piece of you. I knew you'd come for her someday, and I was right. You belonged to me. You were supposed to be with me. But you went and let *him* knock you up . . . with twins yet!"

"I was sixteen years old. The two of you passed me back and forth like a concubine. You disrespected my parents, my faith, and my Native American heritage. Why would I ever let myself be bound to a man who treats women like animals?" Malika seethed.

Cameo's mind reeled. A quick glance at Camille showed her she was just as baffled.

"Jared never loved you," the General went on. "You were nothing but his whore on the side. He was never going to leave his wife for you. He told me so. I'm the one who loved you."

"You? You never loved anyone but your soldiers! And Jared *did* love me. He was going to marry me until you got involved. You blackmailed him into doing your bidding. Neither of us had any say regarding the girls. You threatened my freedom and Jared's career with your bullying."

"None of it matters now," he grumbled, looking at the floor. Then his head jerked up and he glowered at Malika again. "I still love you. Despite the wicked wench that you are, I never stopped loving you. Yes, I took you away from Jared. He was a spineless prick with a wife, a swine who took advantage of a young girl. I may not have done things right. But I have always loved you. And I vowed that you and Jared would never find your way back to each other."

"You're evil!" Malika cried.

"You didn't think so when we killed Jared, did ya now?"

Camille gasped then clasped a hand over her mouth. Cameo stood back, watching this play out.

"Malika pressed harder. "If you loved me, why'd you split up my daughters?"

"To torture Jared. He knew how much I wanted you. He knew about my war injury. But he got you pregnant to spite me, to show me that you'd never be mine. So I made sure you and he would never be a family with your precious twins. He took what I loved so I took something of his."

Malika became silent for a brief period. Emotion brimmed in her picturesque doe eyes. Then she quietly asked, "If you wanted a piece of me, why did you send Cameo so far away?"

"Every time I looked at the girl all I saw was Jared. Her blonde hair and blue eyes . . . she looked nothing like you. I began to hate her. She became a constant reminder of what he gave you that I could not."

"And that's when you turned your military housing into a human trafficking hub, isn't it?" Malika was really calling him out.

An insolent smirk twisted his thin lips. "At least I spared your bastard girls from that. I could've made good money off the pretty little brats. But I figured that would push Jared over the edge and he'd spill his guts about everything."

"Like how you locked me up during my entire pregnancy and fixed the paternity test?" she taunted. "You have no soul."

"Don't preach to me, *Squaw*. You were in no position to raise the girls."

Malika's eyes turned black with rage. "Tell them. I went to

a lot of trouble getting us all together. I want them to hear the truth from the bastard who ruined their lives. I knew they wouldn't believe me. How could they? We've only just met. Tell my daughters what you did!"

"Or what?" he responded with a mocking laugh.

She pulled a gun from inside her jacket and pointed it at him. "Or this . . ."

The General looked around the small gathering. His arrogant expression shifted to one of fear. "Fine. Not that it'll change anything at this point." His attention went to Camille first, then settled on Cameo. "You'd be idiots to not have figured it out after hearing all of this, but I'll appease your mother anyway. I'm not a father to either of you. Yes, I'm guilty of everything you heard here . . . only because I love her more than anything. My jealousy over her torrid affair with Jared turned me into a madman. Your mother has a knack for driving men to the brink of insanity."

Cameo heard a clinking sound and looked toward Shook who'd just cuffed Missy who sat on the floor.

"Daddy!" whined Missy. "Help."

"General Fritz, you're under arrest for the murder of Congressmen Jared Connor and for human trafficking. I'm sure the DA will add more charges to the list." Shook stepped forward and flashed a badge, then began reading the man his rights while roughly flipping him around and slapping metal cuffs around his wrists. Then he turned toward Malika. "Malika Rain, you're under arrest for —"

Before he could get the words out she fired two shots into the General. The man let out a howl of pain as he went down with a thud. He writhed on the floor in agony. She hadn't wounded him enough to die.

And on Cameo's next breath chaos ensued. She heard footsteps pounding up the stairs and down the hall. The door burst open and in rushed Ricochet, seven men, heavily armed, stormed the house and the eighth — a Federal Agent no less — was already in the room. Shook . . .

Cameo grasped the reasoning behind Shook's wild face paint. Nobody could ever have suspected he was an undercover Fed. And since they had no idea who would be at today's takedown, he was covering his identity.

Malika pointed her nine-millimeter at Shook. "You deceived me? And used me?" she screamed. A mix of disappointment and fury blazed in her eyes. "You're a cop?"

"FBI Agent Zero. And you're busted, lady," he replied with supreme authority.

"You promised to help me. We were supposed to kill him, not arrest him. You don't understand! He'll be out of prison within a day. He has contacts higher than you can imagine." Her words came out in a panicky rush.

"We know who he is. He won't get free this time. This will go better if you cooperate," Shook warned her. "Lower your weapon."

Time seemed to halt as nobody moved, for fear she'd kill Shook.

"Like hell it will," she snarled then shot the General three more times before anyone could disarm her. And out of nowhere she whipped a small cylinder-shaped device to the floor.

Thick gray smoke filled the room. Shots rang out and echoed off the walls.

Cameo dropped to the floor and scurried over to Camille. "Get down," she told her. "Cover your face." She pulled off her jacket and covered their heads as the smoke clouded the air. She felt her sister trembling and wrapped her arms around her. They huddled on the floor together as war erupted around them.

Minutes felt like hours before the shooting ended and the rancid mist began to subside. Cameo prayed that what Malika had released was not toxic.

"C'mon," Rush's voice greeted her ears. "Let me get the two of you outta here." He helped them to their feet and toward the door.

Cameo glanced back and saw Missy and her father lying on the floor. Blood soaked the carpet beneath their bodies.

"Are they —" She looked up at Rush.

"They didn't make it. Malika killed them both."

She shielded her mouth and nose with her forearm. "Where is she?"

"She got away," he told her. "I'm sorry. It was like trying to shoot a shadow . . . she just . . . vanished."

"What did she blast us with? Are we okay?"

He offered a reassuring smile. "You're going to be just fine. It was only teargas."

"She'll be back." Cameo sighed.

Rush slanted her a puzzled look. "What makes you think so? She's now wanted for four murders."

"Shook. She'll be back for Shook. I saw the look in her eyes. He just became the next man in her crosshairs."

CHAPTER SIX

Cameo stumbled along, clutching Rush's arm with one hand and Camille's hand in her other. Camille seemed stunned and disoriented. She wondered if her sister was flashing back or just reacting to the teargas.

Once outside, they breathed fresh air and immediately, Cameo began to feel better. She turned to Camille who was shaking. "Are you okay?"

"I-I'm not sure." Big tears pooled in her eyes.

The past two months of conflict melted away in that moment of compassion. Cameo pulled her twin into a warm hug. Surprisingly, Camille ardently hugged her in return then buried her face against Cameo's neck.

"I'm so sorry for judging you, for judging mother, and for the way I've treated you since your return. You were unbelievably brave in there. You stopped that man from striking me and took the pain yourself. Then even after all you heard, you threw yourself over me to shield me from the chaos." She lifted her head. Tears streamed down her cheeks. "I am so proud of you. I couldn't be more honored to have a sister like you. Can you ever forgive me for the way I've behaved?"

Cameo couldn't withhold her own tears. She hated to cry but this was the most heart-wrenching moment of her life. A moment she had prayed for when she found out she had a twin.

She framed Camille's face between both hands and stared into her eyes, as if looking into a mirror. She fought the urge to break down and sob. "All is forgiven . . . *and* forgotten, my beautiful sister," she murmured through tears, her voice quivering.

They fell against each other in a tender embrace and sobbed.

Rush stepped away. "I'll be right over there with the guys. Seems the two of you could use a moment."

"Thank you," Cameo said softly.

After several intensely emotional minutes that would be forever etched in her mind, Cameo eased back. "Are you hurt?

Camille shook her head. "Just shaken. You saved me. Mother called me to meet her here. She said we were going to tell the General who the traitor in Shade's troop was and let him deal with Rebar to keep Shade out of it. She seemed sincere so I went along with it. I never had reason to fear Missy because she was on our side back then. But when I walked through the door, she appeared hostile, and I had no idea why. She led me to that man. I told him who I was, but he laughed, didn't believe me. I tried convincing him that I was Shade's fiancée and that Malika asked me to come. He became irate. You walked in just in time. He was going to beat me to death . . . those were his words." She paused with a lingering sob. "He said, I'll teach you for killing my Joanie. I'm gonna beat you to death and nobody will ever know you existed, just like I planned." She stared back at Cameo with a mix of terror and sorrow. "That's why you panicked the day we met? You knew. You were right about him."

"Yeah . . ."

"Oh, Cameo. He thought I was you. I feel awful for not believing you."

"Thank you." She drew a deep breath and exhaled. "He's gone now. Thanks to mother, actually."

"Our mother is confusing."

Cameo mustered a smile. "Just a little. But she was right

about one thing, and though Ricochet may not agree, Malika knew the old man would pull strings to avoid prison. He would have been out in no time to continue his reign of terror."

"How are you so calm?" Camille blinked in shock.

"I don't know. I've been praying a lot lately. Maybe I'm just relieved that man is no longer stalking me. Maybe it's because I met the most amazing group of men. I don't know."

"Speaking of men. How do I tell Shade the man he admired most is dead at the hands of our mother?" Then a look of shame washed over Camille. "I've done a lot of horrible things in the past year. Things I never thought I'd do. Like helping Joan and Missy kidnap Shade. Helping Malika push Rebar into breaking up with you. Gosh. Treated you like an enemy. How do I move past this?"

Cameo nodded toward Rebar who was leaning against his car while Ricochet worked with law enforcement to secure the area. "He looks shattered," she said. "Maybe a good place to start would be apologizing to him."

"Are you still in love with him?"

"Probably." Cameo shrugged. "But I've moved on. Rebar is hard not to love. He's a sweetheart who got caught in Malika's web."

"Guess I got caught in her web, too. I can't believe what I've done. Rebar will never forgive me."

"Don't underestimate him. You still own his heart."

"You're much stronger than Mother thought," Camille said. "After what we put you through . . . we destroyed your relationship with Rebar . . . a Damocles man. Yet, you're encouraging me to go to him."

"I can only make suggestions, Camille. The ultimate decision is yours. Shade or Rebar? I don't know Shade. I'm not sure why he was doggedly loyal to that man. How well do you know your fiancé?"

"I've known him for a year or so. He's a good man but I've never really understood the thing with the General. They never met the guy . . . yet would not defy him in any way. And anyone who did so became their enemy."

"Like Rebar?" Cameo arched one brow.

Camille nodded. "All the men who sided with Rebar became enemies to Shade. I don't understand it. But I stay out of it. I focus on my new career and let Shade deal with matters regarding the troop."

"Not much of a troop left, is there?"

"No. Just Shade, Jackson, Ammo and Bullet. Once they find out their commander is dead, who knows what'll happen?"

"Did Shade really support your spy mission with Malika?" Cameo pried.

"Yeah. Shocking, isn't it? I think he has a soft spot for our mother."

"*That* could be dangerous."

"He was furious that someone had exposed the General's whereabouts."

"Sounds like you were caught between him and Malika. Both had a different agenda and used you as their tool."

"I knew that," Camille admitted. "Malika wanted him dead, and Shade wanted to warn him. I think I failed Shade, though, because I never found out what Rebar was up to. He vanished rather quickly."

"Rebar's a smart guy." Cameo glanced over at him. Their eyes met briefly. She wondered what he was thinking.

"He is. Shade knew Rebar had something to do with outing the General. Plus, he stole most of Shade's friends."

"He didn't steal them. They're grown men who made up their own minds."

"Even so, Rebar led the way to rebellion. Shade's gonna want his head over this disaster. And now the General is dead."

"The man was a wanted criminal. He ran a human trafficking ring." Cameo bristled. "Whose side are you on? I'm starting to get mixed vibes."

"Shade's my fiancé. The tryst with Rebar was an act, something mother and Shade asked me to do. I must admit, I enjoyed it though. We got really close to uncovering Rebar's secrets, too, before he caught us."

Cameo was glad she hadn't blurted out anything about *Face Palm*. The conversation seemed to be shifting like a hurricane. "I'm confused. You just apologized and asked how to move forward. But you still sound loyal to Shade's cause. What about Rebar? Don't you feel bad for what you did to him?"

Camille did a non-committal-nod-shrug thing. "I feel bad for coming between you and him. That was mother's idea. But I had to find a way into his den to get what Shade wanted. The only way to do that was by seducing Rebar into believing I wanted him."

"You just said you wanted to make things right."

"We did, didn't we?" Camille hugged her again. "I'll be forever grateful for what you did in there. And I hope we can get to know each other."

"Me, too." Cameo pulled back to look at her. "I guess it'll take time for us to sort all this and get our lives back on track."

"You think I should talk to Rebar before I leave?" Camille asked.

"I'm not sure now is the right time. I was under the impression you regretted playing a part in that whole thing."

"Oh, I do! I'm so sorry for causing the breakup between you and Rebar. That was a horrid thing for me to do. Now that this is behind us, you and he can work things out."

Cameo scrunched her brows. "I'm not with him anymore. I'm with *him*." She discreetly pointed to Rush who stood a few feet away talking to Rider and Stoke.

"Which one?" Camille glanced over.

"The guy wearing sunglasses and a cross necklace."

"Mm, yes. He is a hunky one." She gawked at the gathering of men. "Who's the goth one . . . the guy with really long straight hair and smokey dark eyes?"

"That's Rider. One of our eight."

"Hm. A group of hotties for sure. Wow. I see why you moved on so quickly."

"I didn't choose to. After Rebar dumped me, I left Colorado. Things just kinda happened naturally with Rush. It's not serious yet. He knows I'm rebounding and struggling with trauma."

"Ohhh . . . do you have PTSD, too? From what the General did?"

Cameo nodded slightly. "In Santa Fe, yes. When he and his daughters took us captive . . . when I killed Joan."

"Gosh. You are a brave woman. And a fast thinker. I'm so glad you got rid of that lunatic woman." Camille paused and stared as if thinking, then added, "You must be filled with relief. The General can never hurt you again."

"And . . . he was never my father. I can't even put into words how good it feels to finally know the truth about our birth, why we were separated, and the paternity."

"Oh . . . wow . . . that's right." Suspicion flickered in her eyes. "Jared was *your* father, too. I wonder why he never mentioned it."

"I can answer that," Shook said upon walking up to them. "Sorry for eavesdropping but when you mentioned paternity it caught my attention."

Camille took a step back. "I remember you. Malika brought you to the house. Were you her boyfriend? Why is your face painted?"

Shook evaded the question about his face. "Malika asked for our protection today. She wanted her daughters to know the truth and she made sure there were witnesses so nobody could call her a liar."

"Do you know why Jared never claimed Cameo as his daughter?"

Shook gave a brief nod. "When Jared decided to change his will and tell you both the truth, Malika and the General conspired to kill him. Jared wanted to meet his other daughter and include her in his inheritance. But your mother didn't want a scandal that would draw attention to her. It's a long story and one that would be best told by her. I've already said more than I should have."

"My father wanted to meet me?" Cameo stared up at him, wondering what that would've felt like, to meet her real father.

"I'm sorry, babe. So sorry for your pain. I can't imagine what you're feeling right now." He leaned forward and kissed her cheek. "We're here if you need us."

"Wow . . ." Camille sighed. "Looks like you're one of us after all."

"Huh?" Cameo whisked tears from her cheeks.

"You have a troop of your own. Mother was wrong about you. She said *I* was the only one like her. That *I* was the only other woman men couldn't resist. But look at you, sis, with a troop of eight wrapped around your finger."

Cameo chose not to argue. "I think you're still in shock. How about you apologize to Rebar before you leave."

"Are we going somewhere?"

Cameo glanced toward the house where police were wrapping things up for now. Yellow tape sealed off the estate. "They're about done here. For now, anyway. I'm going back to Dallas. That's where I live now. I assume you'll be heading home to Shade?"

"Yes. I'm afraid to tell him what happened."

"He probably already knows," Shook told her. "We'll wait

69

for you by the bikes, Halo."

A flash of jealousy traversed Camille's face. "He calls you *Halo*?"

"They do, yes."

"That was the name Shade gave *me*."

"You can blame Rebar. He's the one who started calling me Halo and it just stuck. We're not in competition, you know. I'm not after your man, not even Rebar. You can have them both, though I doubt the Damocles brothers would share."

"Never know," Camille huffed then marched over to Rebar.

Cameo followed at a safe distance, unable to resist listening in. After all, her twin had exhibited several shifts in personality in a short span of time. For reasons that eluded her, she needed to know what transpired between Camille and Rebar. He was part of Ricochet now, which Cameo deemed a privilege.

Camille would never know he'd slipped *Face Palm* onto her. Everyone on the outside assumed that Ricochet found the General this time via Malika. After all, she'd initiated the meeting. Cameo was relieved that today's incident had nothing to do with Rebar or his tracking device. Perhaps Shade would back down on his pursuit of the so-called traitor.

"Rebar, are you okay, baby?" Camille asked in a sugary tone.

"I'm not your baby," he said without looking up from his phone. He closed the device and tucked it inside his coat. "Get what you came for?"

"Um . . . not really. Did you?"

"I was just here to help my new friends."

"Oh. Well. I came over to apologize," she said.

He lifted his head and stared blankly at her. "For what?"

"For causing the breakup between you and Cameo. Maybe you can patch things up."

"Doubtful."

"Well, if you don't wanna get back with her then how about coming home with me?"

He let out a short sardonic laugh. "And do what? Share you with Shade? Oh wait, you didn't get what you came for so now you're afraid to go home to big bad Shade. Maybe you wanna seduce me again to try and orchestrate another search through my office."

"That was all my mother's doing. This is me talking now. Mother took off and who knows when or if she'll return."

He pushed off his car and stared down at her. Lines on his face drew taut and his voice was steady. "Fool me once, Camille . . . you know the cliché. I thought I was in love with you. I wrestled with those feelings for a year while you shacked up with Shade. Then out of the blue you tricked me into believing your engagement was off and you wanted to marry me. So like an idiot, I threw away the best thing that ever happened to me only to find out a few days later that you'd lied. That you were still engaged, and I was just a pawn in some twisted game you, Shade, and Malika conjured up."

She grabbed his arm. "Why did you give her my name? I'm Halo, remember?"

He wrenched his arm free. "Because she *earned* it. You may have been Shade's Halo, but you could never be mine. Why am I not surprised that's all you care about?"

"You love me, Rebar. You can't deny it."

He turned and opened his car door then looked back at her again. "I love your sister. Real love . . . the real Halo. Not some fantasy like I had with you. But she's with someone else now and I don't blame her one bit for separating herself from all this mess. Even so, I'd still rather be in love with her and help her recover than waste one more minute obsessing over you." He slipped behind the wheel of his Gran Sport. "Not sure what you came for but can't say I'm sorry you didn't get it.

Go home, Camille. You're not welcome in Ricochet." He slammed his door.

Chamber trotted across the yard, shot a heated glance at Camille then jumped into the passenger seat. The car rumbled away.

Wow. Cameo stood there, watching the gleaming black car fade into the Amarillo sunset. *I couldn't have said it better.*

Camille strolled over to her. "I tried. He's still angry over what I did. I better hit the road. I've got a six-hour drive back to Colorado Springs."

"I'm surprised Shade let you drive all that way alone, considering the circumstances."

"He really wanted answers and mother stressed it was important I come alone." Camille shrugged. "I just don't know what to tell Shade. I'm glad you and I met again. Thank you for saving me."

"You're welcome." Cameo smiled a little. "We're full sisters, you know. There's no longer that lingering doubt over paternity. However, I remember what you told me about Jared, it sounds like he was remorseful in the end and tried to do the right thing. It feels kinda good knowing he wanted to meet me."

Camille gave her a probing look. "Jared was scum. The only good thing he ever did was leave me his inheritance."

"That's more than the General ever did for me. Then again, I was never his." Cameo felt displaced.

"Are you going to sue me for half the inheritance?"

"Sue you? You're my twin sister. Why on earth would I do such a thing?" Cameo's brows knitted in disappointment.

"People do strange things for money. Just so you know, Shade has the best attorneys. I wouldn't try coming after my money if I were you. I'm still trying to get my business off the ground."

"I don't want your money. I have an impressive resume

and intend to further my career. That's why I moved to Texas. Besides, I've never been about money."

"Oh . . . good then. We won't have to deal with that."

"Isn't Shade a billionaire or something, though?"

Camille nodded. "I don't want to become dependent on him. People will think I'm marrying him for his money."

"Is that why you've not set a wedding date?"

"Partly. I'd really love to have my new career booming before marriage. I've always been independent. Mother approved of my decision. She said never to depend on a man."

"Shouldn't love for family come first? Is Shade okay with waiting?"

"He's getting impatient. He wants children before we get much older. Not sure I want kids. Do you want kids?"

"Never thought about it. I'm nowhere close to marriage," Cameo replied.

"Ha. You may be closer than you think. Look at that troop of hot men over there waiting on you."

"We refer to ourselves as family, not a troop. We aren't militants. Ricochet's purpose is much deeper than that of Shade's former troop. We don't bow to some demented invisible boss."

"Rebar said I'm not welcome with them. Why not?"

Cameo had trouble grasping her sister's audacity or maybe just sheer lack of consideration for anyone but herself. "A few reasons. Your loyalty to Shade and Malika presents a risk to us. What you did to Rebar, and how you treated me, was deceitful and calculated. Ricochet is about compassion and helping others, not destroying people."

"So you're telling me that I'm not welcome in your new family?" Agitation hung on her voice.

"You have a family of your own. You deliberately kept me away from them and never welcomed me into your life," Cameo said as gently as possible. "Then you reconciled with

73

Malika after telling me you wanted nothing to do with her, and you conspired with her behind my back. Your actions are confusing, and at times very hurtful."

"I thought you said all was forgiven and forgotten," Camille said with a pout.

Cameo sighed. "I'm trying, hon. Really I am. You're not making it easy. Like I said, it's going to take time. You might want to start by pulling your jealousy under control and stop throwing out the digs."

"I guess . . ." She looked away then at her car. "I'm gonna get going. I'd like to be on the Interstate before dark so I don't get lost in this dreadful town."

Realizing they had major obstacles in the way, Cameo agreed it was a good time for her twin to head on home. She was mentally and physically exhausted and tired of defending herself.

"I hope you have a safe drive home," she told Camille. "Once the dust settles, maybe we can get together."

Camille swept her hair back. Her gaze met Cameo's who read a strange expression in her twin's eyes. Almost one of challenge . . .

"Maybe," Camille said, then walked to her car and left.

Cameo gazed after her sister. It was as if an icy arrow had just pierced her heart. *Maybe?* Was everything Camille had said completely fake? Trying to force her suspicions from her mind, she headed toward the group of men, her family . . . It was time to go back to the place she could finally call home . . .

CHAPTER SEVEN

Rush forked a stack of Ribeye steaks off the grill onto a plate then carried them to the table on his patio. Everyone had just taken a late-night swim in his pool. Afterward, Cameo said goodnight and went up to bed. He didn't fault her for wanting some alone time after the day they had endured.

"Hey, doesn't get better than this." Rider was first to grab a thick juicy steak. He spooned potato salad onto his plate.

"Thank God for takeout," Stoke said while filling his plate with side dishes Rush had picked up on the way home.

"Got any hot sauce?" Moss asked.

Rush pushed a bottle his way. "You're gonna ruin that perfect steak?"

"Nah, mate. Gonna make it better," Moss teased.

He watched his family grab platefuls of food then find a comfortable place to sit. He felt blessed to have inherited this incredible home. He'd worked hard to keep everything in excellent condition. After everyone had their food and a spot to sit, he filled his plate and plopped into a cushioned chase lounge beside the pool.

"It's really good to be home." He sighed contentedly, while slicing off a piece of fine steak.

"How's Halo doing?" asked Chamber, who sat next to Rebar.

"She's got a lot on her mind, but otherwise, I think she's doing well," Rush replied. "Wish I could've been in there when she stood off against the old man."

Shook nodded in agreement. "I wish you had all seen her. Damn. The moment she heard a whip crack she practically bowled me over to get into the room. She snatched that thing from him in the blink of an eye then lashed him straight across the face. I've never seen a braver woman."

"Hot damn." Rider sighed longingly. "I can just picture her standing there in that black leather biker outfit, wild blonde hair, brandishing a whip over the bastard. Rush, you are one lucky man."

Rush couldn't withhold a little chuckle over his friends gushing over Cameo.

"She's a kitten and a wildcat. Today she was a wildcat," Shook told them. "She kept that whip trained on the old man while Malika pried the truth from him. Then when Malika dropped the teargas, Halo rushed to her sister and shielded her. She didn't think twice. She simply leapt into action. Despite the gunshots and chaos, she kept her head. I do believe she overcame some demons today. Her switch from victim to victor simply blew me away."

"You deserve her, Rush," Rebar said, much to everyone's surprise. "I'm glad she found you, and your family. This family is a much better fit than Shade's troop could ever be."

Rush's eyes widened slightly. "I'm impressed. You may fit in here after all."

"Rebar's a good man," Chamber said. "He got caught in the web of a couple of dangerous women. He didn't mean to hurt Halo."

"I get it." Rush gave Rebar a nod of acceptance. "Stick with us, Rebar. We're on the winning side."

"Thanks. I hope Cameo agrees with that one day," Rebar said.

"Might help if you don't call her Camille again." Stoke scoffed.

Rebar rolled his eyes in open regret. "Yeah, that was a bad

slip. Their names are so close."

"Just call her Halo," Stoke suggested. "That's who we know her as. She's Rush's angel. Did anyone tell you about the little angel girl and how Halo helped Rush survive the bullet wound?"

Rebar nodded. "Chamber filled me in. And that she took one hell of a beating to protect my secret tracking device."

"Then just call her Halo."

"Got it." Rebar looked around the group. "Thanks for welcoming me into your family."

Rush eyed him carefully for a few moments, then said, "You're welcome. But you're still a probie"

"Fair enough." Rebar lifted his drink in submissive salute.

The others raised their bottles in approval.

"I hope the probie becomes permanent," Levi said. "I heard from Hunter this morning but didn't wanna tell you until after the mission."

"What's up with him?" asked Rush.

"He's decided to stay in Australia. He fell in love with the rescue and married her. He said he'll give you a call once things settle down."

Rush glanced toward the house. "It happens." Then he looked at Rebar. "Maybe your timing is spot on. Not to mention you bring valuable skills to the table. I'm sure Halo will come around in accepting you as one of us now."

"She will," Shook added. "I overheard her with Camille this morning. She still cares about Rebar. She persuaded her twin into apologizing."

"And did she?" Rush wanted to know.

Rebar shrugged. "In a strange sort of way. She was all over the place, said she was sorry for breaking me and Cam . . . Halo up, then she asked me to hook back up with *her*. No way am I getting involved with that mess again. I set her straight on how I feel."

"He did indeed," Cameo said from the patio door. "Any steak left for me?"

"Hey, angel," Rush stood up to greet her. "Thought you went to bed."

"Couldn't sleep. The delicious aroma of those steaks made my stomach growl."

He prepared a plate for her. "Come sit with us." His spirits rose just at the sight of her.

All the guys stood and began clapping in unison.

"What's this?" she asked, her cheeks blushing adorably.

Rush glance around. "Shook filled us in on your heroic actions. We are in awe."

"You're all very kind but I didn't do anything extraordinary. When I heard the whip, something inside me snapped. I have no idea where that burst of courage came from."

"Right here," he laid a hand over her heart. "You're a natural warrior, a true member of Ricochet. You really are the angel we needed to complete our family of renegades."

Tears glistened in her lovely blue eyes. She dabbed the corners with dainty fingers. "Thank you. I'm a bit overwhelmed." Her gaze swept around the group. "Everyone's here. This is nice."

Rush took her hand and guided her onto the roomy lounge chair with him. She dug into her food with zeal as the guys chatted. Nothing had ever felt this good to him, having the perfect woman to make his house a home.

"I thought you didn't cook," she teased. "This is delicious."

"I didn't cook. The grill did," he bantered. "The rest is take-out."

"Did anyone catch Malika yet?" asked Cameo between bites.

She caught Shook and Rush exchange an apprehensive glance.

"Don't be afraid to tell me," she told them.

"We're not afraid," said Shook. "Embarrassed is more the word. How she evaded eight fully armed men mystifies us. It's like she vanished in a cloud of smoke after she launched the teargas."

"I warned you not to underestimate her."

"That you did."

Rush noticed a peculiar expression flit through Shook's eyes that nobody else would've picked up. But he knew his friend. They'd been close comrades since before Ricochet formed.

"She got under your skin, didn't she?" Cameo asked Shook in her typical no-nonsense manner.

Apparently she read Shook better than Rush thought. Perhaps his beautiful angel was more perceptive reading the guys than any of them realized.

Shook hesitated with his reply as if searching for the right words. Or maybe he wasn't even sure himself, Rush quietly observed.

"I'll admit this was one of my more difficult assignments," Shook began. "During the time I spent with Malika, she poured her heart out to me, said she could finally tell someone everything because she had Ricochet's protection." He paused, clearly choosing his words carefully. "There were moments when I felt sorry for her. The pain she endured from the tender age of sixteen . . . I have a hard time wrapping my mind around these cases at times."

"She's a survivor in her own bizarre way," Cameo said.

"Yeah," he agreed. "On the other hand, she bears all the earmarks of a sociopath. I'm sorry to say this to you, being that she's your mother. But I won't lie to you about what I know. Malika is extremely dangerous, just as you said. If she ever reaches out to you again, I gotta warn you, Halo . . . stay away from her."

Cameo sighed sadly. "She hates me that much, huh?"

"I wouldn't use the word hate," he replied. "Just that her thought patterns shift constantly. She's completely unhinged. What I do know is that nobody is exempt from her playbook of tools."

"Which basically means she'll use anyone as a means to an end, even her daughters. Is that what you're trying to say?"

"More or less. I'm sorry, doll. I wasn't going to bring her up, but you seem to want answers."

"It's okay, Shook. I appreciate your honesty." Cameo set her empty plate aside. "I've learned a lot about my past since she dragged me to the States. While it hurts to know the truth, I'm glad to have answers to questions I've had all my life."

"You're stronger than Malika thinks," Shook told her.

"Thanks." She smiled a little then became serious again. "Are you in love with her? Did you fall for the infamous Malika Rain?"

"No," he replied without a hint of doubt. "Did she get under my skin at times? Yeah. I felt her pain. But I heeded the warnings and stayed the course. I know agents who've lost their way undercover. I'm lucky. I have this family to keep me grounded. So, no, sweet Halo. I have no feelings whatsoever for your mother. She's a callous criminal who continues digging deeper holes for herself and I won't rest until I slap cuffs on her dainty wrists and lock her up."

"I'm glad to hear you stayed strong." Cameo still sounded worried. "You do realize she'll be back, don't you?"

"She'd be a fool to come out of hiding," he said with a disconcerted look.

"Like you said, she's a sociopath. Now that the General is out of her way, she'll set her sights on you. You betrayed her trust. She views men as public enemy number one."

"We'll be ready," he said.

"Wait . . ." She looked up at Rush from her position at his side. "Remember I had a strong feeling that Malika and the

General were scheming together?"

"Yeah. But she shot him. What are you thinking?" Rush asked.

"She smoke-screened us. I've replayed my conversation with Camille all day and how she acted afterward. Malika said she wanted Camille there for us all to hear the truth together. But what if . . . what if the whole meeting was to draw Ricochet into the open?"

"What purpose would she have in doing that?" Shook asked.

All the guys moved closer, clearly waiting to hear Cameo's suspicions. Cameo sat quietly for a second. Rush saw her thoughts coming together.

"It's Shade," she said. "Malika has wanted him since the day they met."

Then Rebar spoke up. "I never told anyone this. I was sworn to secrecy by Shade. Way back when Halo and I started dating, I had a brief conversation with Shade and asked him about Malika. He referred to her as a *Native American goddess* and *dangerously seductive.*"

As if suddenly onto something, Cameo gestured for him to say more. "You mentioned something in that direction to me earlier. Spill all of it, Rebar."

Rebar let out a growl. "Shade said he'd kill me if I ever breathed a word of that conversation."

"We're waiting, man," Rider prodded.

"Yeah," Stoke chimed in. "You're part of our family now."

"Shade told me that despite being chained to a pole and watching everything she did, that Malika aroused him . . . to put it delicately," Rebar told them. "She struck terror into him with her ice yet turned him on with her fire. I asked if he'd get involved with a woman like that had she not been a criminal, and he said possibly."

"Whoa, that's a shocker," Chamber said. "Why didn't you

ever mention this to me?"

"Shade threatened to kill me. Besides, you know I don't go back on my word. Well, except this time."

"Then it's possible that Malika and Shade have been privately meeting," Cameo said. "From what Camille said, Shade is furious that Rebar left and took half the troop with him. He sent his own fiancée into another man's bed as a spy. What does that say about the man?"

Rush thought back to his chat with Cameo and realized she'd been onto something all along. "Seems if Shade was seriously in love with Camille, he'd never let her sleep with another guy. And that his vendetta against Rebar is more important to him than his own woman."

"Or is *she* really his woman?" Cameo arched a skeptical brow.

The guys sat in stunned silence. Rush observed their faces as they processed this unexpected possible turn of events. If this was the case, he wondered when Malika had decided to target Ricochet and use them to help her take out the General. Had she also used Cameo to get rid of Joan?

Levi, who was typically the quiet one of the group, expressed his thoughts. "Sounds like Malika decided she wanted Shade. Set Camille up to go after Rebar to pave the way and when things didn't go as planned, she and Shade came up with a new plan."

"Which is what?" asked Moss.

Levi shrugged. "I haven't got that far yet."

"Oh my gosh. That makes sense," Cameo agreed. "And I played right into her hand. Her whole victim routine was merely a ploy to spy on Rebar and hook him up with Camille. She lured me back to America just to use me because she knew her other daughter was too loyal to team Shade to go up against the General and his daughters."

Shook's expression saddened. "That sounds about right

from things she told me. I couldn't tell you, though. I'm having a hard enough time watching you deal with everything else."

"I wonder what Shade and Malika are up to next?" Rush sat back, rubbing his chin meditatively.

"Well," Shook began. "Thanks to my failed attempt to arrest her, they now know Ricochet has an undercover Fed in their ranks. We've lost the element of surprise. I figure they'll step up their game plan."

All eyes turned to Rush for his response. He draped one arm around Cameo's shoulders, leaned back on the chaise and placed a tender lingering kiss on her forehead while contemplating everything.

After a few moments of thought, he gave full attention to the best team of men he'd ever worked with. They were his friends, his family, and loyal comrades. Not a man among them ever bowed to fear. Rush raised a toast. "Then so will we, mates . . . so will we. Let the games begin!"

Each face displayed a satisfied grin. They lifted their drinks in cheers and salute, confident in their ability to defeat even the most cunning enemy.

"Here's to us!" Stoke cheered.

Everyone nodded in unity, even Cameo.

"To Ricochet!" reiterated Rebar.

Rush was happy to Rebar settling in, and even better that Cameo seemed more at ease with his presence.

Someday — maybe — he'd tell Rebar that they were brothers. But not tonight. And not tomorrow. They had a war to win, and his half-brother needed to earn his rank.

Yet he couldn't help but feel the beginning of a bond, something he'd never thought possible when they first met. But now, Rebar was beginning to look and act more like Ricochet and less like Shade.

Rebar had definitely chosen the right family this time.

Read what happens next in Feather Blue: Book 7

ABOUT THE AUTHOR

Shiloh is a bookworm who grew into an author. Writing has been a way of life for her since grade school. She majored in English, graduated and eventually found success with a few good publishers. January 1, 2016 Shiloh officially went Indie. In her words, "The only time I'm truly free is when I'm writing."

As a survivor of hardship and chronic disease, she takes one day at a time and treasures the simple things in life. Shiloh is a Christian, loves animals and practices being kind and generous every day.

Her achievements include The Golden Wings Award for her debut novel The Satellite, the UK Nobel Pin and Editor's Choice Award for her poem The Lonely Man, numerous 5 Star Reviews from Fallen Angels Reviews, InD'tale Magazine, and other professional reviewers for novels published under former pen names.

Her novel Forever in Darkness became a finalist in the 2017 RONE Awards.

Her novel *Chained Reaction* earned her third 5 Star Crowned Heart Review and a nomination for the RONE 2021 Awards.

Writing stories you'll live in!

www.SusanZoeBella.com